"Suzanne, you're becoming a lady now," said F. Parnell Manfred, principal of Robert E. Lee High School. "You should cast aside silly ball games and turn to less aggressive, less tomboyish pursuits. If you must be a sports fan, why not join the cheerleaders?"

But a special fire burned within Suzanne Hagen and she wanted nothing to do with cheerleading, baton twirling, folk dancing, or any other "feminine" activity at school. She wanted to play ball; and if boys could play football, why not girls?

R. R. KNUDSON grew up in Virginia, attended Sidwell Friends School in Washington, D.C., earned a B.A. from Brigham Young University, an M.A. with honors from the University of Georgia, and a Ph.D. from Stanford University. She has written an English text with Arnold Lazarus, edited *Sports Poems* with P. K. Ebert, and written many articles on schoolbook censorship, as well as reviews of sports books.

THE LAUREL-LEAF LIBRARY brings together under a single imprint outstanding works of fiction and non-fiction particularly suitable for young adult readers, both in and out of the classroom. This series is under the editorship of Charles F. Reasoner, Professor of Elementary Education, New York University.

ZANBALLER

R. R. Knudson

For my mother,
who always let me play,
and for Wyatt,
who didn't

Published by
Dell Publishing Co., Inc.
1 Dag Hammarskjold Plaza
New York, New York 10017

Laurel-Leaf Library ® TM 766734, Dell Publishing Co., Inc.

ISBN: 0-440-98819-5

Reprinted by arrangement with Delacorte Press
Printed in the United States of America
First Laurel printing—August 1974
Second Laurel printing—July 1975
Third Laurel printing—January 1978
Fourth Laurel printing—August 1978
Fifth Laurel printing—December 1979

Chapter 1

Wham chug!

  WHam chug!

  WHAMChug!

WHAMCHUG! WHAMCHUG!

  WHAMCHUG! WHAMCHUG! WHAMCHUG!

  WHAM   WHAM   WHAM   WHAM   WHAM

WHAMWHAMWHAMWHAMWHAMWHAM

WHAM SSS S S S S s   s.

At 9:45 that Indian summer morning I raised my head off the desk where I had been snoozing. I'd finished the first monthly exam early and hoped to rest up for the big volleyball playoffs that afternoon. I poked Rinehart across the aisle. He kept writing like a cyclone.

"What's that noise, Rinehart? It woke me up. I've got to be fresh for the tournament."

He wrote on, ignoring my "pssst" and "Come on, Rinehart," and other assaults on his attention. He probably wouldn't notice me if a king cobra was biting my jugular. Old Fuzzy looked over my way, so I slumped down in my chair and thought about the game.

Volleyball, the dolts' game. Even seventh graders play it to perfection, jostling and chittering as the too light, too white ball loops over the net for a gentle reception. Serving that pasty blob always makes me think of smacking an uncooked spudnut, and who

wants to slug a potato donut? Plus rotating, nudging
over from one position to another. For some reason
even our stars could never remember which way to
move. Ech! Still, volleyball is better than being in
sixth grade, where our back-to-school sport had been
tetherball. I won't bother to describe that "sport," fit
only for infants. It's one baby step this side of shuffle-
board. Yes, volleyball is better than both. And it could
be played on our old warped gym floor. But soon,
basketball! Basketball begins next week. That happy
thought made me sit up straight again.

Or was it the WHAMCHUG?

WHAMCHUG!

WHAMCHUGWHAMCHUGWHAMCHUG
WHAMCHUGSSSSSS S S S S S S S s s s s s   s.

Down the hall, somewhere over near the gym, the
noise began again. WHAM! WHAM! WHAM! Slow
at first, and then faster and hissy. Unbelievable. My
teeth gritted. My ears began to ring. Even Rinehart
looked up. Other kids stopped writing and eyed each
other. Throughout the term our weekly quiz had
been accompanied by power mowers zzzzzing under
the windows. That southern humidity never helped
your grades, either. Ninety-five degrees at the blackboard, mower blades throbbing outside, and Fuzzy
had struggled one month with two and a half parts of
speech. One full month of underlining, circling, filling in the blanks. Oh, those adverbs. Would we ever
get on to interjections? WHAM! WHAM! WHAM!
But this was worse. Even our fuzzy teacher looked up
from her newspaper.

"Just keep working," she said.

"The noise interrupted her funnies," whispered
Rinehart as he wrote. "She's fuzzier today than usual.
Look how her overwrought permanent stands up."

But only the hair. Miss Harrison didn't get up. She

kept looking from the door to the funnies as if she expected to find an answer to the WHAMCHUGs right there in *Peanuts*. Or *Dick Tracy*. He'd discover the sound polluter.

"Just go on with your tests. Is anyone finished yet?" She'd given up on the noise.

No one spoke. I pretended to be checking over my answers, noticing that as usual I'd forgotten the heading. I scrawled "English 8, Monthly Exam I, Zan Hagen" and poked Rinehart for the date.

"Drat it. Can't you see I'm busy?" He scribbled another page.

WHAMCHUGWHAMCHUGWHAMCHUG
WHAMCHUGWHAMCHUGWHAMCHUG
WHAMCHUGWHAMCHUGWHAMWHAM
WHAM!

Louder and faster now. My knees jiggled. The noise vibrated the floor sending gross chills to my temples and jaw. Fuzzy glanced at the clock. She's gonna skip *Pogo* and collect our papers, I thought. Writing "I solemnly promise that I never gave nor received help on this test" under my name, I started to get my books ready. The ringing bell mingled with WHAMs, freeing us for third period.

"Maybe it's a runaway lathe down in the shop."

Laughter.

"Must be a bulldozer."

"Sounds like a steam shovel."

"Or Coach O'Hara in the shower."

Laughter.

"Fifty thousand pile drivers."

"More like a pneumatic drill," said Rinehart, trying to keep up with me.

"A moronic drill."

"I can't stand much more of it."

"Could be blasting down a wall."

"Or ripping off a roof."

"Or taking up a floor."

"If it doesn't stop I'll scream."

On the way to chorus I overheard kids speculating on the racket. Rinehart shouted over the noise:

"You see, I didn't know a thing for that exam. Drew a complete blank. Couldn't find one adjective. Did you find any 'ings' anywhere? What did you match them up to?"

"Then what were you writing all last hour?" I hollered.

"Stayed up all night reading *Siddhartha*. Wow, it's dynamite!"

"Try *Sporting News*. Much better."

"Underlined some great passages," he said, pulling the book from his back pocket and reading.

"But what were you writing?" I persisted.

". . . But how will he, who is so hard-hearted, go on in this world? Will he not consider himself superior, will he not lose himself in pleasure and power, will he not repeat all his father's mistakes . . ." He panted. I didn't.

"But what were . . ."

"Didn't underline any adverbs. Hesse doesn't use many. I circled some adjectives and nouns, though. Remembered them from last year. What do you think of 'Gotma' for my dog's name? Or 'Krishna-Agi'? How about all those symbols Hesse put in there? See for yourself." He started to hand me his marked-up *Siddhartha*. I tried again.

"Then what were you writing?" I screeched again, just as a blistering noise stopped and we arrived at the chorus room. Miss E. won't take any goofing off, so we quickly mounted the risers, opened our music, and hummed a few bars while waiting to begin. Behind me the basses and baritones flipped pages and

mumbled lines of Latin. We went on to the French
national anthem, then some madrigals. Finally the
bell rang and Miss E. put down the stick and freed
us from the carrot-smiles. We had only a sec to speed
over to science.

"Did you notice how the noise stopped for Miss
Elliot? That woman's a magician."

"What were you writing on the English exam all
period?"

"Tell you at lunch," said Rinehart, disappearing
in a crowd toward the science wing. On his way to
advanced-placement biology, he had no time for a
lowly general science peon—me. I felt glum and hun-
gry.

I hate science. It's worse than tetherball. About
the only things I could ever understand were the
names and dates of the scientists. I passed with a "D"
by memorizing my notes. They didn't make sense.
And I could never see anything under the microscope,
although I could watch a curve break over the plate
even if thrown a hundred miles an hour by a twelfth
grader. No pitcher could fool me. But the microscope
did. Through it everything looked like a moldy bad-
minton shuttlecock. I gave all my oral reports about
the lives of the scientists, about how Isaac Newton
hated his children and how Galileo was a crabby hus-
band. Last year in general science I got by with a
term paper on the marriages and divorces of Nobel
Prize winners: "Did the discoverer of vitamin B love
his wife?" I asked as a thesis question. The teacher
had written, "What has this to do with cell reproduc-
tion?—'D'—Try harder next time." That helped.

Just now the class was discussing projects for the
annual science fair. I sort of half followed the discus-
sion.

"Are there any questions?"

"How many words?" a girl behind me asked, and then everyone chimed in.

"Does it have to be in ink?"

"When is it due?"

"How many pages?"

"Will you accept late projects?"

"Does spelling count?"

"Can our mothers help?"

"I can't type."

"Do you want illustrations?"

"I can't draw."

"Can I count the title in the number of words?"

You know, the really crucial questions when one talks about science. I tuned out and sketched a poster I planned as my project. It was to show the many uses of the sphere. I lettered, "The sphere is a solid geometric figure, generated by the revolution of a semicircle about its diameter," copying the notes that Dr. Semler had dictated from Funk and Wagnall's. "It's a round body whose surface is at all points equidistant from the center." Then I drew under this lettering a marble, ping pong ball, golf ball, hand ball, jai alai ball, squash ball, billiard ball, tennis ball, lacrosse ball, baseball, softball, polo ball, boccie ball, tetherball, volleyball, beachball, bowling ball, and worked up to that super ball—basketball. What shall I do with a football, I puzzled, and was about to ask when a gigantic WHAMWHAMWHAM! clanged through the room. The class became chaos.

"I'm not going to shout over that tumult," shouted Dr. Semler. "Just take the rest of the period for a study hall. See me after school about your projects."

"It's almost lunch time anyway," said the boy who couldn't draw.

"What time is it?" asked the girl who couldn't type.

Five seconds to meatballs. I hurried to the cafeteria

and spotted scrawny Rinehart holding our usual two seats. We loners have to stick together. I plunked down the brown-bag lunch I'd carried around all morning.

"You save my place, I'll get our milk, okay?" I headed for the line without waiting for an answer. By now all WHAMs had stopped. I heard someone ahead say he thought that "the machines are at work in the gym." What machines? He did say gym? No whirlpool bath can make that much commotion. Or the time clock. No other machines down there. I bought fudgesicles and Hershey bars. Dr. Semler had explained how sugar raised your blood count and energy level. I'd need muscle for the tournament. We might go six games or more only two hours from now. Wish it were basketball.

"Ick. I've begged Mom not to wrap my sandwiches in old bread packages," said Rinehart. "It's disgusting. And I can't take tunafish again."

"Now lookit, Buster. You're gonna tell me what you wrote for one solid hour on that English exam."

"Couldn't I read you some Hesse? I can't confess while eating soggy Little Friskies on stale bread. All right. All right. Listen to this—"

I opened my lunch and settled back comfortably with roastbeef on rye. Blood-meat. Energy for intramurals. I expected a pitiful confession from Rinehart about how he begged Fuzzy, in a tearful letter, for a make-up exam, of how he told her that Siddhartha's problems with his parents touched him so deeply that he was unable to circle a single adverb. I expected also his embarrassing plea that I understand and forgive his brownie note to Fuzzy. After all, he forgave my silly obsession with sports, didn't he? He was coming to watch me play ball today, wasn't he?

No such luck. As soon as Rinehart began in his confident tone I knew he'd won again. He wiped off his thick glasses on a paper napkin as he explained.

"So anyway, I just sat there and wrote a long letter to my grandmother. 'Dearest Grandmother,' I said, with a perfect comma following that friendly salutation. I had even the inside address and margins all correct. And another comma after the complimentary close, 'Your loving grandson, Arthur.' "

> Arthur Rinehart
> 17-14 Glebe Road
> Arlington, Virginia
> October 1, 197-

Dearest Grandmother,

I am sitting here in English after positively breezing through a monthly exam for which I studied all night. I would not have needed the twelve hours extra study either, because I have kept up right along. Grammar has been so much fun this year. We're learning the exact same things we learned for the past four years, but Miss Harrison really brings it to life while she diagrams sentences. She tells little jokes and gives us cute short-cuts for detecting nouns. She's pretty, too, in fact my best English teacher ever—except you, Grandma. Thank you for sending another book. I've always wanted to read *The Adventures of the Little Wooden Horse*.

So now that I have scored 100 on my exam I have lots of time to tell you all the events that are happening at the *maison* Rinehart. (I'm working hard in French, too, and expect my first report card next week to be all A's.) Right after this period I shall go to the office and mail this letter so it will reach you just in time for your

Golden Wedding anniversary. I love you, Grandma. And now about the family . . .

He paused, swallowing a Twinkie in one mouthful.

"Then I turned that letter in when the bell rang. It's up in Room 201 in that messy pile now, and since grades are due on Monday, Fuzzy should get around to reading it maybe Sunday night after she watches *Bonanza*."

"But your real exam! Where . . . ?"

"Over in my locker. I'll finish it perfectly in study hall, using the green workbook, of course. At 4:00, after your play-offs, Champ, I'll buy a stamped envelope and send the exam airmail to Grandma. No sweat."

I clutched my head and swayed against the table. "You . . ."

"When Fuzzy discovers my hasty error she'll tell me to have Grandma send that test directly to school, to Old Dimwit down in the office."

"And of course you'll ask Fuz, in your Sunday-school voice, glasses slipping oh-so-boyishly down on your nose, if she would mind sending your letter to Grandma. You'll even hand her a stamp." I was furious with admiration.

"How did you guess?"

"You creep, Rinehart. If you weren't such a clumsy creature—if you could throw a ball more than four inches or even catch one—you'd be an all-round genius."

"Well, we are alter egos, aren't we? Even if I am older. So you throw and catch for me."

"I will. And soon."

Chapter 2

Thursday afternoon dragged as it always did. My dog of a history course, taught by a mean man, came first. I hoped for WHAMs to drown his surly lecture, but all remained calm. Then came study hall, that Tuesday-Thursday substitute for gym class. Not my idea of a substitute, mind you. Our gym wasn't big enough to handle all the kids at Robert E. Lee Junior-Senior High School. Not big enough, plus the old floor was badly warped. So some of us cooled our heels in study hall twice a week. I usually read whatever novel Rinehart put into my hands, but today I worked out a volleyball game plan. Our team would start right out with our best server and with our three tallest players at the front. We'd establish control of the net: that was the thing. And we'd hold serve as long as possible, thus building up an early lead and great confidence. Confidence is all. Yes, E. J. would start serving with Putt at the net. I drew a messy chart positioning our players while I watched the clock tick sluggishly. True, my home room wasn't loaded with talent, but we'd made it this far. If we could slip by 10-6, I was sure we'd knock off the eleventh graders. And then 12-2—they were so apathetic this year. But big. Intramurals weren't all that bad.

Finally I put my head down on the desk and dreamed about basketball. One more week to go. Then varsity practice began. We would get new uniforms. I saw myself making fifty-foot hookshots and ten for ten from the foul line.

"Let's go. It's time, ball player. Come on, Zan." Rinehart jabbed me with his slide rule. We pushed our way through the bus lines, racing for the gym.

"Meet you in the stands after the tournament," I said. "I'll go with you to the post office." He ducked into the boys' locker room, shortcutting to the bleachers, as I pushed the swinging door of our locker room.

Every bench sagged with girls in various stages of suiting up. Every one of them seemed to be crying, their sobs mingling with the sound of showers running and the loudest WHAMCHUGs yet. Girls sat, completely dressed in street clothes, blubbering and red-eyed. Others had gotten as far as loafers off, sneakers on over heavy wool socks. They'd gone no further except to pull handkerchiefs, into which they now bawled. A group by the shower stalls had gym suits on but not buttoned. Only Teeny Miller was in full uniform. She used her pinny to weep in. I glanced around, looking for a body that could answer questions, when just then Aileen came out of the shower, dripping, but not tears.

"I didn't need a shower, but since it's our last day in the locker room until April, I took one for Auld Lang Syne," she said over the wailing, and started to dry off.

No one budged. The gloom was thick enough to cut with a hockey stick. For a whole minute I just stood there.

"What's going on around here?" I flung open my locker and tossed in ball-points, books, shoes, game plan. I hoped someone on my own team might notice their captain. "What's going—" A titanic WHAMCHUG drowned my words. Sounded like drilling or . . . WHAM . . . right next door in the gym.

"We hadn't heard the news either till just before you came in," screamed Aileen. "It's the gym floor, you know." The noise stopped.

"No, I don't know, but whatever's the matter can't be as gross as all this sniffling." I took my clean gym suit carefully off its hanger and stepped out of my skirt.

"No one told us till we got here," said Teeny, starting to put on her skirt.

"Told you what?" I waited, blouse in hand. I hung it up. "Told you what?"

"Mrs. Butor came in about five minutes ago to report that we wouldn't be playing volleyball today."

"Or basketball next week," added Aileen, dry and dressed again. "The warped old gym floor is being torn up. A new one will be installed just in time for the softball season—March. She did say March, didn't she? So that wrecks the winter prom. And I'd hoped to be queen."

Suddenly the locker room became absolutely silent. I could even hear the bells of the Good Humor truck in the parking lot. Everyone watched me. For a second I simply held on to my sweatshirt and stood still. Then I leaped for the gym door. They must be kidding me. I slammed through and out onto the courts.

Or what was left of the courts—now a sports disaster area. The floor was a shambles, gaping with monstrous holes. Piles of jagged, ripped-up slivers, recently our floorboards, filled the back court. Picks, axes, sledgehammers, claws littered the front court. Huge green trash barrels bulged with plaster, bits of bricks, empty sardine cans, and pop bottles. Against the wall, volleyball nets sagged helplessly around their poles and tires. The vaulting horse lay on its back, filling up with nail kegs, bags of concrete, trowels, levels. The trampoline, jammed in row "D" of the bleachers, was powdered with fallen plaster. Climbing ropes were knotted and flung over the rafters. Only the basketball nets remained intact, floating uselessly above the crater. The time clock winked crazily: home team—zero.

Sprawled on the tumbling mats, hardhats took their afternoon break. Several appeared to be asleep. One of them knocked off a Mountain Dew. Another was eating Fritos while he tried a few sit-ups.

"Hey, girlie, is this how it's done?" he called to me, his uncoordinated motions more like frantic waves from a drowning man than like exercises.

My eyes fastened on an old guy leaning on his pneumatic drill. He seemed to be their foreman. I picked my way over to him. Shaking with rage I kicked a Yahoo bottle out of the center circle and said, "WHY?"

"Why have you done this? Why today? Why now? Why here? What are you doing? What are all of these guys doing here? Don't you know we've finally got the gym to ourselves for a tournament? See—the boys aren't here. It's all ours." I waved at the ransacked courts. The foreman blinked. I stepped over some electrical cords and moved closer.

"Who told you to do this? Who could have thought of this?" I pointed to a hole. The old guy edged backwards, pulling along his drill. "If you think you can trip me with that thing, you're crazy. And don't turn it on, either. Listen to me." I unplugged the drill with a savage kick and pointed toward the locker room, my arm trembling, my voice for its first time soprano. "There in that locker room—my team. That room is filled with girls who want to play ball. Even volley-ball. We came to play."

"Wha—?" he finally said, looking around at his de-molishers, who now stared from me to him.

"Did you remember that basketball season is com-ing up? Could you believe that I've waited a whole year for next week's call out? Have you ever heard of the *Herald* Tournament?"

"What?"

"Why did you do it?"

The sit-up guy, breathing heavily from three flubbed attempts, rolled his Frito bag into a ball and shot at the trash barrel. He missed. He stood up.

"It's just our job, girlie," he panted. "We don't mean you no harm."

"It's just your job to tear down Lee gym? What kind of a job could that be? You are heartless."

"The floor is warped, foundations crumbling. This here ancient place is dangerous. A little girl like you could break her neck. Now, take off." The foreman spoke at last as he bent over to plug in the drill again.

"Your job? What could that mean? My life! You've ruined my life."

WHAMWHAMWHAMWHAMWHAMWHAM WHAMWHAMWHAMWHAMWHAM! The foul line disappeared into a widening hole. A workman yelled over the din.

"Don't you think you better put your shirt on, girlie?"

Chapter 3

Black Friday. Like a zombie I made my way from class to class. Rain fell all morning, splashes as big as golfballs knocking at the windows. No one heard thunder because of the continuing bolts from the gym. Lightning shot through a mournful sky, reminding me of the speed with which dreams go awry. Winds howled between WHAMCHUGs, ebbing to a sigh as our English class arrived at the library. We were all to select something for a book report and had orders from Fuzzy to "Spend the period looking around carefully while I correct your exams." She left for the teachers' room. Rinehart had brought his own novel. "*Demian* won't be there anyway," he said. "The librarian hates Hesse."

I flopped into one of the two easy chairs and read the newspaper. Dirty water, dirty air, fires, crashes, murders, putsches, revolutions, wars—so what? Come out and see Lee gym, you reporters, if you want to look at international tragedy. I thought of how it would look in color on the front page of the *Herald:* SEASON ENDS FOR LEE GIRLS: BALLGAMES OVER AS GYM REBUILT. Overhead camera shots of workmen playing frisbie with a yellow hardhat. Group portraits of half-dressed girls crying, hailing the cameraman with their pinnys. A zoom shot of redheaded Aileen wrapped in a pink towel: "Where will we hold our winter dance?" the beauty who might have been mistletoe princess sobs. Then a close-up of a short, pugnacious ball player, fist shaking in front of her blue eyes: "Team captain Hagen socks it to hardhats. Workmen driven from court in flurry of left jabs and uppercuts. Interviewed at craterside, foreman claims 'a five foot shirtless blonde bomber' broke his nose with blow from a Dr. Pepper bottle." Wide-angle views of deflated volleyballs and basketball backboards draped in black bunting.

I looked up from my imaginary front page in time to see Fuzzy come back and take Rinehart out into the hall. She's onto his trick, I thought. Look out, Grandmother. Watch it, Rinehart. They stood talking by the door as the loudspeaker blared for the fourth time that day.

"All boys. All boys. If it is raining during your P.E. period, report to the stage of the auditorium. Otherwise, report to the football field as usual. Girls. Girls. The gymnasium is under repair. No one is to go there for any reason. Repeat, *any reason whatever*. All girls report to room 324 for your physical education class until further notice."

Where is room 324? What could be going on there, I wondered, briefly, turning to the sports page. I'll find out soon enough. Now headlines and captions rose up from the newspaper to mock me. It seemed as if all girls, everywhere in the world, became sports champions overnight. Except, naturally, those banished to room 324.

"Girl jockey rides five winners at Hialeah. She boots home Manny Boy, a 100-to-1 shot." And there she was, pictured in her silks, whipping her nag to a photo finish. No tacky bloomers on that one, I thought, remembering my seventh-grade gym suit. And what a great cap she's got there.

"Soccer goes sexy south of the border as women's world cup play-offs reach Mexico City." I read as far as "Lavender dressing rooms are complete beauty salons, uniforms multicolored with hotpants." What about their speed, footwork, and a few scores from old Aztec Stadium next time, I grumbled, darting a quick look at Rinehart, who appeared to be ashen-faced.

"First woman admitted to garage area of Indianapolis 500 plans to become racer." She sat atop a Porsche saying, "I hope to reach Sebring this year and by summer be ready for Le Mans." What a terrific crash helmet she's got there.

"Australian tennis queen reaches finals. Nineteen-year-old miss from down under wins 6-1, 6-1 in swift decision." I'd even take that sun visor, but did she have to wear top-to-toe lace to make Wimbledon? Rinehart came my way. I finished the sports page.

"Iowa girls begin long basketball season. State tournament in Des Moines their goal." I scanned a picture of satin-suited players, all of them about eleven feet tall. "Will one of these lovelies be drafted by the San Francisco Warriors?" asked the caption. I checked them over, willing to predict that even if they were all spastics they would join the Boston Celtics if their heights were taken into consideration. I hated being short. I wished I was that girl on the end, the tallest one in the picture—about 13-9. Or if I could be as tall as Rinehart! I wished I was in some Iowa corn belt beginning the stretch drive to state finals. Instead, there I sat in Northern Virginia, listening to a pneumatic drill razing my future. I wanted to be dead.

Rinehart tapped my shoulder. I looked up at his smile. "All's well, Zanner. Fuzzy bought my story and then went down to the office to mail my letter to Grandma."

"Then why were you white and trembling?"

"Faking it, naturally." He turned back to Hesse and I to my sports headlines: "All girls, everywhere, sports heroines."

I couldn't sing at choir practice. I kept seeing those piles of devastated floorboards. I kept choking, croaking. In science class I said good-bye to the spheres. Nothing can come of a ball project, I reasoned. It will only break my heart. Instead I'd try to renovate my *Julius Caesar* "culminating activity"—a model of the Globe Theater I had made last year. I'd used 700 sugar cubes. I'd convert it to a replica of the house in which Madam Curie fell in love with Mr. Curie. I hoped none of the other trillion Globe-makers came up with the same idea. Let them refurbish their model guillotines left over from *A Tale of Two Cities*.

Then I went to eat lunch at The Blue and Gray, a ramshackle candy store about a block from school. I couldn't eat with Rinehart. I couldn't take his jokes about the gym. I knew I'd ruin my tennis shoes on the way. Sloshing through mud puddles never helped canvas. So what? Who needs gym shoes in room 324? Yet I ran all the way to keep in shape.

I recognized no one at The Gray. Older kids, a few greasers playing pinball, motorcycle types shoving dimes into the jukebox. Not exactly athletes. I ate my Hydrox, drank a chocolate milk, and bought a few chocolate B.B. Bats for good cheer. I studied the bulletin board.

"Drummer wanted for Fridays and Saturdays. Boys, call RA 1-5488 to join small band." Say, maybe I could advertise for a gym that the girls could use. There's the YMCA, the Police Boys' Club, the Pop Warner League gym. Arlington has plenty of boys' gyms. But how would we all get there, miles away. I chewed and plotted. I looked out the window, noticing a few boys on the field tossing a football around in the rain. They didn't seem to mind puddles. Why couldn't girls play football? Why couldn't we have a field instead of room 324? I looked back at the bulletin board.

"Purchase season tickets for basketball away games. Support your team. Let's go, Generals." I scribbled "What Season?" and started looking at the rest of the graffiti. Some wag had penciled, "Manfred is a creep," and other less delicate dumps on the new principal. I didn't know the guy. Had never seen him. I'd only heard his voice over the loudspeaker. True, he bungled the daily announcements. He can't pronounce and sort of lisps. But could he be the perverted beast that these scrawlings suggest? What did he think about the gym? I'll bet he could figure out a way to save the girls' basketball season. He's the principal, after all. I know, I'll skip history next period and go to his office. I'll demand—no, ask,—no, *beg* him to help. I felt much better as I shivered through the rain.

I had been waiting in the outer office for five minutes before a secretary noticed me there among kids seeking late passes, bus passes, sick passes, and change for the hall phone.

"You're too late for a sick pass." She shook her head. Her curls jounced. "And we haven't any more change."

"I'm not sick, I'm not late, I don't need change. I want to see Mr. Manfred."

"Your name?"

"Zan Hagen."

"Your grade and section?"

"8-3. May I please see Mr. Manfred?" A few truants shuffled positions on the bench, looking up at the urgency in my tone. The secretary reached over to answer the phone. After a few hurried "Nos" she came back to me.

"Mr. Manfred is very busy," she said, giving me what she probably hoped to be a discouraging look. "Maybe Monday after school . . ."

"I must see him today. Now."

"Where are you supposed to be this period?"

"At lunch," I lied, knowing she'd send me to history if she knew the truth. I started toward his door, giving the gate of the outer office a businesslike thwam.

"Now just a minute. Where do you think you're going?" She moved to place herself between me and Manfred's office door. I kept walking.

Just then a short bald man emerged from the principal's office.

"Oh, Mr. Manfred, this girl wants to see you."

"Not now. I'm on the phone with the contractor." The secretary looked triumphant. My ears perked up.

"The gym contractor?" I asked. "That's what I want to see him about." He took papers from a desk, turned, and went back into his sanctuary. "Sir, that's what I want to see you about. The gym." I followed him.

He mumbled a few numbers into the phone, then, "March will be fine," and "No, there's no hurry," and hung up.

"Sir, March will not be fine. We need that gym now, today." He seemed at last to notice me. His secretary remained in the doorway.

"That's all right, Gladys. I will manage this girl." She stepped back into the outer office, leaving the door ajar. A long shadow on Mr. Manfred's rug told me she lurked just outside. What am I in for now? He sat there examining me with narrow eyes while I checked out his walls. Behind his desk, a case of trophies gleamed under indirect lighting. State twirling champion Lurleen Dewey held a prominent position on the center shelf next to First Prize, Fife and Drum Corps. Four Southern States Speedball Tournament cups were mixed among Majorette-of-the-Year Citations to Ruby Jean Twilley. The bottom shelf, crowded with debate-club trophies and Yell Queen blue ribbons, looked junky. I strained to read inscriptions while Manfred straightened the coffee cups on his desk. Where are his books, I wondered, making a mental note to tell Rinehart that his principal, the school's intellectual leader, had only one book in his office—the Arlington County phone book.

So now the scene is set. Friday afternoon. Outside: rain, thunder, lightning, and mud. Inside: a wet co-ed in huge, bookless office. Across a tidy desk baldy looks up and says, "Take a chair. Now what's all this about the gym?"

ZAN: Sir, was that the contractor you spoke to?

MANFRED: It's none of your business, but yes.

ZAN: And you told him there's no hurry about fixing the floor?

MANFRED: Of course I did. The gym needs a complete rebuilding, from the foundations up. A big job. Takes time.

ZAN: But sir, basketball practice was supposed to begin next week.

MANFRED: And indeed it will. The boys' team is to be bused daily to the YMCA over in Clarendon.

ZAN: The boys? What about our team. We hoped to play in the *Herald* Tournament this spring. We almost made it last year. Please sir, we need a place to practice.

MANFRED: Say, now I know who you are. You're that crazy little girl who raised such a ruckus with the builders yesterday. I heard about your antics, believe me. Screaming and kicking. Not very ladylike. You forgot your shirtwaist, too, didn't you. Have you no shame?

ZAN: But sir, we were supposed to have intramural play-offs yesterday. And next week basketball practice . . .

MANFRED: Yes, yes. But I felt this to be the right time for repairs. And so did the contractor. The "Y" gym has been made available for practice and the boys will play their games away. I've heard that Lee's a strong team on the enemy's court. A real whiz-bang road show. That so?

ZAN: But sir, what's to become of girls' sports without a gym for the season? We don't even have a field to play on. The boys have it for football.

[*Enter secretary who hands Mr. Manfred a manilla folder. She exits. Mr. Manfred scans contents.*]

MANFRED: Now then, Suzanne. I see here that you are fourteen, almost fifteen. Fourteen years old. A young woman.

ZAN: My name is Zan.

MANFRED: I prefer your given name, Suzanne. Softer, more feminine. Yes, Suzanne, you're becoming a lady now. You should cast aside silly ball games and turn to less aggressive, less tomboyish pursuits.

ZAN: Like what . . . sir?

MANFRED: Well, dear, if you must be a sports fan, why not join the cheerleaders. Classy costumes, a few gentle leaps. Stir up the crowds to cheer for our fighting boys. You'd get to shout into that nifty new electric megaphone.

ZAN: Wear those stupid pleated skirts? Feh! I hate maroon. Besides, cheerleaders don't win anything. They don't score points. They waste their energy.

MANFRED: Twirling lighted torches. That should be exciting enough for you, eh? You'd be peaches and cream as a majorette. Running onto the field waving a gold baton. High-stepping all over the end zones. Like a real live fashion model. I can hear the music now. Lee's Golden Girl!

ZAN: Phoney nonsense. I want to play ball. I like to win.

MANFRED: Competition, that seems to be your drive. Well, then, Suzanne, we have proper ways for a young lady to excel. I note here in your record such high marks in English. Did you know that the county spelling bee comes along next month? Suzanne Hagen, Arlington County Spelling Queen. Oh, your school would gain such publicity from that! I shall place your trophy high on that very top shelf. In your years remaining at Lee you could retire that trophy to a permanent niche right beside me.

ZAN: To stand forever between the Pillsbury Baking Princess and the Embroiderer-of-the-Year. Oh, no you don't. I want to play ball.

MANFRED: Say, you'd look mighty cute in a snappy band costume. You'd get your picture in the *Herald*. Sequins sparkling. Furry tassels blowing in the wind. White boots dancing . . .

ZAN: Dancing is my utter worst thing. And sequins itch. Besides, I can't play an instrument.

MANFRED: Never mind that. Any fool can bang a drum. . . .

ZAN: They never give girls the drum. We always have to play the glockenspiel.

MANFRED: Then bang a glockenspiel. You even have

time left this season to learn the formations. Tricky things, those marching formations. But according to the I.Q. score recorded here, you can do it. I have every confidence that you'll soon be spelling out "Let's Go, Generals" with the best of them.

ZAN: Listen, Mr. Manfred, the only formation I'd march in would have to spell out, "Give the Lee girls a gym." Otherwise that's all drivel. No, I won't march.

MANFRED: Or spell?

ZAN: Or spell!

MANFRED: Or twirl?

ZAN: Or twirl!

MANFRED: Or cheer?

ZAN: Or cheer!

MANFRED: Or . . . ?

ZAN: Or play the Sousaphone. Or try out for the pep society. Or sing in the fall follies. Or join the projectionists' club. Or run for secretary of the student body. Or enlist in the Future Cosmetologists of America. Or change my name.

MANFRED: Now, now . . .

ZAN: And I will not dance!

MANFRED: Hmmmmmm. These psychological tests here indicate such a stubborn streak. You've proved to me that your first-grade measurements are correct. I feel I can be of no further help to you today.

ZAN: But Mr. Manfred . . .

MANFRED: Hmmmmm. I see from the schedule that you're supposed to go to physical education in just a few minutes. Am I correct? My secretary will show you out.

ZAN: Come to that, where will our gym class meet and what will we be doing all period?

MANFRED: Hmmmm. You'll soon find out, but I will

tell you that I've arranged for the girls to have Lee's very largest room, except for the gymnasium which, as you know, is undergoing substantial changes—for the better.

ZAN: Room 324?

MANFRED: Good-bye, Suzanne. Come in for a fatherly chat any time. Gladys, show this obstinate young lady to the door so she won't be late to class. And make an appointment for another photograph for her cumulative record. This ugly one in a sweat-shirt is most unfeminine.

Some father, I thought. Some help. I'm doomed. I slunk off to find room 324.

Chapter 4

Up, up, up. The climb would help me keep my wind. On the third floor landing I passed a group of girls carrying knitting baskets. Needles and bits of yarn stuck out through the wicker. Why would anyone want to bring her mother's knitting to school, I wondered, noting another bunch of girls gazing at a glassed-in display of tatting, crocheting, and crewel work. Several dress dummies stood outside room 316. Paper patterns flapped about their hips. I could only hope the computer wouldn't go berserk some semester and stick me in a sewing class. Or that creepy principal. He's just the type to exile me to a full year of flax spinning. That's dainty enough for him. In room 318 sewing machines whirred. I paused to watch a prissy teacher threading a bobbin. I hope she pricks her finger and the whole building goes to sleep for five months. "Sleeping Ball Players," they'd call it. Except the workmen—they would keep at it. Then when we woke up the gym would be ready for basketball season.

"Somebody stole my pinking shears!" A frenzy broke into my dream of the mossy home economics department with its cobwebby looms. Yes, that's where I was, the home ec wing. No wonder I hadn't seen any boys. They were lucky to be down in the shop and outside at football practice. But zounds! What could a P.E. class be doing up here with the

ncedles and thread? I hurried now, almost colliding
with a refrigerator that someone had pushed into the
hall. Its door gaped, revealing a shriveled head of let-
tuce and a lidless jar of mayonnaise. Must be left over
from that semester E.J. spent learning to make Wal-
dorf salad and lime Jello. I began to see myself in a
track suit, standing before a Tappan range. I was
tapping my cleats while waiting for the oven timer.

And then, behold, room 324. Yes, indeed, the sec-
ond largest room in Robert E. Lee Junior-Senior
High School. The cooking-class room, Arlington
County's largest kitchen.

But no ordinary kitchen today. Stoves, refrigerators, dish cabinets, tables had been pushed against
the walls, leaving a vast playing area cluttered with
only a few sinks. Probably these were immovable.
Boxes, hampers of baking pans, cookie sheets, Jello
molds, silver, and Tupperware lined every space between the appliances.

"Not quite a scene from *Good Housekeeping,* is
it? Greetings, cooking mate." Teeny Miller came out
from behind the broom closet.

"Well, we're obviously not going to cook or the
ovens would be hooked up. Anyway, it's gym class.
Where's our teacher? Who's in charge here?"

E.J. looked up from a cookbook. "She's probably
trapped down in her office. Have you seen the gym
floor today? Worse than yesterday. I ate lunch with
the foreman and found out that there's no hope for
our basketball season. The earliest they *might* finish
is February."

"And I've just come from old Manfred's palace. He
went and deliberately sabotaged our season. He hates
girl athletes. Wants us all to be cheerleaders and sing
fight songs for our brave footballers." I retied my

shoes, ready to play. There seemed enough space for calisthenics and skill games, maybe even tetherball.

"I wouldn't be surprised if Mrs. Butor had a hand in annihilating our season," said E.J. "She's never liked to coach basketball. She detests staying after school. Now that I think of it, she's the only gym teacher in the world who actually dislikes sports. When I was a seventh grader she told our class that she'd majored in dance and the sole reason she taught sports was that dancing couldn't be put into the curriculum. Not enough demand."

"I've heard she's a mighty bowler. Tops in the teacher's league. Lowest handicap on Lee's team." I retched.

E.J. got up and did a few jumping jacks. "The floor isn't bad. Good traction." She tried out the door frame. "Good support. We'll use it for chin-ups."

"She's supposed to be good at Ping Pong, too. Probably her dancer's training." Teeny took a mop and waltzed with it to the door. Girls kept coming in, everyone doing a double take on seeing the disarray.

By a stroke of good fortune, probably a computer error, many of Lee's best athletes had been scheduled for this class. Coming at the end of the day, it became a catch-all class for hard-to-schedule kids. We had eighth graders through eleventh graders. Real ball players. But lazy. They mostly had to be prodded to come out for the teams. Here they sat now, doing homework or watching football practice from their high grandstand on the stoves. Phyllis Badger—a junior, finest foul shot in the county. Twenty for twenty. Regularly. Swished them in under game pressure, too. Millie Murphy—for a large girl she ran well, next to E.J. the speediest forward. Junior Joan Sterne—a little slow afoot but master of the zone defense. No one dribbled by her. She knew how to get in their way, legally. And Bumpy—hot hand from half-court. She drove the guards crazy with twenty-foot set shots. Her shooting eye might have taken us to the *Herald* Tournament this year.

"Let's get going," I said, trying to pull the gang away from their gossip session. "Take five laps around the kitchen. Do a couple of knee bends to get the feel of our new gym . . . Come on." A few rose, touched their toes, and sat down. Putt faked a shot at an open bread drawer, then turned back to the window. E.J. and I started doing sit-ups. She banged her head on a sink but kept going. One by one, the gang joined us. Then ten minutes after the bell, arranged in businesslike rows, we all tried some pushups. Except for Aileen. She wasn't about to mess up her hair exercising. She peered at us over a teacup of water.

"You make me feel soiled just watching you. How can you grovel around on that nasty linoleum?" She sipped prettily. Manfred should be here to see this. She's his type.

"If you won't exercise, make us all a cup of tea. You can be the team tea queen," said E.J., jumping in place. "We'll soon be thirsty."

"One, two, one, two, one, two, one, two," I counted, leading a line of joggers around the sinks. Maybe we could hire a plumber to remove the pipes and push these into the sewing room. They'd work for tie dyeing. We'd hold a cake sale to pay him. Things were definitely looking up. "One, two, one, two . . ."

"Gals, gals, gals, gals. Why the uproar? Why this tromping?" Mrs. Butor called from the hall. "Someone come out here and help me with this phonograph!" She trudged wearily toward us, lugging a stack of records and a worn briefcase. Books poked through its torn seams. She gasped for breath, winded, no doubt, by the three flights. That and being overweight. Sloppy fat, that gym teacher. She couldn't make that climb all day, I thought as she sank onto a sink.

"Come on, you guys, keep at it," I yelled, still galloping around the room.

"Gals. Gals. Stop this at once. Your actions are completely out of place in this kitchen. Stop it now. Answer while I call the roll. Phyllis, Aileen, Eleanor, Suzanne . . ."

"Oh, oh, she's been talking to Manfred. She's never called me that name before," I whispered to Teeny, who was unpacking the briefcase. I tried to read book titles over her shoulder. *Folk* something. Dust jacket picture of feet and musical notes.

"Now girls, as you know, we won't be using our gymnasium until spring." She smiled broadly. Her eyes lit up. "But fortunately, we'll have it in time for the softball season."

"And the tennis season. And golf. Hot dog!" I said in my worst sarcastic voice. Mrs. Butor ignored me.

"So I thought it would be fun as well as entirely right for this feminine setting . . ." She paused and swept her hand around the room, ". . . in this genteel setting to try something different, an entirely new skill for our bodies." She looked down at herself in a red polka-dotted dress. Its full broomstick skirt covered several boxes of kitchen utensils. She took a few dainty steps to her right. The cookie sheets rumbled.

"What could she be up to in that peasant costume?" Teeny pondered, handing me a book—*Folk Dancing for Beginners* by Hulda von Blixon.

"Yes, gals, today we begin to dance. You're going

to love it. Are we all ready?" She scanned us and hopped to her left.

Down the hall I heard a needle drop. No, it was right here—the phonograph needle. Music began. Battle stations, everyone. Right full rudder. Fire one! We have met the enemy and it's our feet.

Chapter 5

The grim details of those endless October dance sessions still haunt me and perhaps always will. Mrs. Butor began with "something simple to get your feet in dancing rhythm." The polka. We went on that first day to the Finnish reel, the Norwegian March, and the Swedish ring dance—a sort of smörgasbord of lunacy.

"Monday, gals, the Highland fling and the oxen dance. Maybe even the crested hen. Now hands on hips, everyone. Hop left, touch top of right toe to side. Hop. Hop. Isn't this fun? Hop. Hop. Hop right. Touch top of left toe to side. Come on. Hop like in hopscotch." She giggled.

"She is insane," I said to my partner, E.J.

"Hop. Hop. Join hands and hop, hop, hop. Very nice, gals."

"She is sick."

"Suzanne, you're not dribbling a ball now. Don't hunch down. Stand up and hop."

"I can't believe it."

"Well, in some ways it's better than suiting up and getting all sweaty," I heard a hopper say.

"Just you wait. You'll need a shower after the Russian cossack," said E.J., hopping to the left.

"Stamp forward right, heels together. Stamp forward left, heels together."

To my right about four inches a stove loomed. Not too much stamping to be done in that direction. I

lunged out of the way of a runaway stamper, nar-
rowly missing a trash basket.

Mrs. Butor started watching me. "Don't worry,
Suzanne, if you knock over a basket we'll use it for
the Mexican hat dance. Ha ha."

"She is a very sick woman," I said, wanting now to
avoid all small objects at any cost. E.J. shook her
head, agreeing with me—or was that motion part of
the reel?

Mrs. Butor was still watching me, hopping and
stamping in my direction. By now, red-faced, eyes
bugging out, straining for breath to shout her orders,
she looked like a reject from the Calgary stampede—
worst in show.

"One smiles as one dances," she huffed. "Enjoy, enjoy." She jigged around me, noting first my feet,
clumsy in my basketball hightops, then my face,
which must have been a frightening sight. I was dis-
gusted.

"Put more of yourself into it. Come on. Slide. Close.
Repeat. Point your toe. Slide. Close. Repeat."

"She must be utterly mad," I mumbled to a toe
pointing at mine.

"Smile and slide. Smile and slide." She broke into a
huge grin. "Isn't this lovely? Come now, isn't this
more delightful than your old ball games? Smile and
slide."

All at once I did a nutty thing. I bolted across the
room, sliding perfectly into third base—the small rug
in front of a sink.

"How's that for a slide?" I smiled up from the
floor. "I beat the throw from the catcher and may
even steal home."

"Suzanne. You are fourteen years old. That is hardly dance etiquette."

"But we aren't dancing. We're hopping and stamping and sliding. I passed this course in third grade."

"Get up off that floor. You are insolent, in addition to being the worst dancer in this group. The worst I've seen all day. No—in my career."

"How would you know. You haven't seen me dance yet. We're not dancing."

"Oh, very well. Tomorrow we'll square dance."

Did she mean that square dancing was real dancing? She's a moron along with her insanity. A mental midget. Yet Monday we did square dance, and Wednesday and Friday. Unbelievable. Worse than that, some of the kids began to *like* "dancing." "Anything's better than ball," a partner of mine said about halfway through a twenty-minute promenade. I stamped on her foot and tried to think of some way to sit out the rest of the period. I sulked.

The wheezy phonograph played thick black records of "Coming 'Round the Mountain," "Red River Valley," "Alabama Jubilee," and "Hinky Dink" while we danced the Texas Star, Birdie in the Cage, Dive for Oyster, Dip for Clam. Mrs. Butor served as caller.

"Promenade completely around the ring. Now all do-si-do with partners. All allemande left with your corners. Forward and back. Ladies, grand chain. Gents to the left."

By now half of us wore pinnys. We were "gents" doing the crossed-hand swing, the right-and-left-hand star.

"Can't tell the dancers without their pinnys," she'd say as we pulled them on. Gross! In a stupor of sashaying I planned a shooting. They shoot dancers, don't they? I ran through several schemes to blow up the dance floor. If only the stoves were gas instead of electric. How about that hot-water heater in the corner? That would explode. I danced over there, only to find it disconnected, like everything else in the room, including the teacher. Maybe a fire would do it, I thought, weighing my chances of getting into the building that night. I wonder if enamel and formica burn. I could push some sewing machines in from the next room. They're in wood cases. And those dress dummies would burn. Maybe Rinehart would help me bring in kerosene.

"All join hands and do a four-hands-round." She purred now because about half the class was playing along with her. Who knows, maybe they go for dancing. Fools. "Not so much body contact. We're not playing football here."

Satisfied in a week that we had mastered the rudiments of square dancing, Mrs. Butor appeared Monday with her next trick. I might have known she was up to something, since for the first time she wore a raincoat while making out the absentee slips. E.J. rolled her eyes upward, a quick prayer for a ball dance.

"Okay, gals and gents, you get a break today. You'll sit this one out. He he." No one laughed, but I almost fainted with delight. We lounged against the appliances. I shot a victory "V" at E.J., who had managed to have herself appointed to run the phonograph for two days in a row. My turn would come.

"Tap dancing has been staging a comeback, and some of us who are tappers couldn't be happier."

"So it's to be a lecture," I noted to the gents around me, wishing I had brought along *Sports Illustrated*.

"Today I want to show you what real tapping is and then Wednesday we'll all try it." Before I could raise a hand to make the protest that might stave off a debacle, she removed her raincoat. Lo, that bovine body was stuffed into a midnight blue tuxedo, a fake one with a skirt. She grabbed a cane off the refrigerator and said, "E.J., start the music."

Only then did I notice the black patent-leather tap
shoes she wore, now awkwardly flopping to "You're
a Grand Old Flag." No one moved. No one even tit-
tered. Was it the shock of seeing an aged Shirley Temple there by the sink, tapping as if there were no
tomorrow? Her bow tie bobbed on her Adam's apple.
Were the kids as embarrassed as I? I couldn't look at
her. I studied my grubby fingernails. I relaced my
hightops. I checked the ceiling for cracks. I tried to
curl my bangs with my index finger. I checked the
floor for warping. Does linoleum warp? Please let it
warp immediately. I strained to count cars going by.
I shut my eyes, waiting for the bell to ring. Please
ring. Why isn't anyone laughing? I looked around
again. Could it be that these kids admired—no, enjoyed—no, *wanted* to learn to tap? She's winning
them over. Well, she's not going to get me to tap. I
will not tap!

"Buck routine," she shouted over the tubas. She
grabbed a top hat from the counter. I crept toward
the door. "Military routine. Note how I end on the
balls of both feet."

"What could she know of balls," I mimicked,
creeping along the wall.

"Rhythm buck or broken buck routine," she called
over "Stormy Weather." "Brush left, slap left, ball
tap, tap, tap."

I felt myself exploding with laughter, with tears.

"And now for the shuffle. Oh, if only we had a
piano up here!"

I inched open the door and crawled out into the
hall.

"Left toe tap, brush right, repeat left, three heel
taps, in place. I love it. I love it. Hitch kick. My legs
actually pass each other in air with a scissors motion,
knees straight!"

I nudged the door shut and leaned against a locker. I could still hear an eerie "Give my Regards to Broadway" and fading click click clicks. I will not tap. I sat like a stunned soldier, Henry Fleming up against the wall, until the buses wheeled into the parking lot. Then I went home.

I skipped P.E. Wednesday. For the first time in my life I skipped it. I went over to Readmore Bookstore and flipped through *Sports Afield*. Nothing but hunting. They should get a new title—"Killing Afield." On the phone that night E.J. reported that tapping had caught on big.

"You must be kidding." Yet I knew she told the truth. The class seemed to be enjoying "dance." "I'm skipping Friday, too," I said. "Don't wait for me."

"But Friday we're not going to tap. We're going on to something 'more important.' "

"What could that be?" I asked, planning to get there early enough to insist on taking charge of the phonograph.

"Search me. See you then."

Friday's class began with a great opening scene. "I'm really going to perspire today, gals. Let's raise the windows and invite in the cool air." Dead leaves blew in. Ashy smoke from a pile burning beneath the window started to fill the room. Mrs. Butor called our names while we speculated as to what was under her raincoat this time. It was clasped tightly around her neck.

"What's a tutu?" I heard from Teeny, who had captured the phonograph. She sat with three feet of records piled next to the speaker. We were in for it.

"Oh, grand, the smoke will be symbolic," said Mrs. Butor, sliding out of her raincoat while pulling a long mauve scarf from the pocket. She stepped forth in a

pink leotard. Feh! Ugh! I'm seeing a pink elephant.
I squirmed in place. What now? I tried to catch a few
eyes, all at once noticing crepe paper everywhere—
huge gold bells taped to the counters, pink streamers
hanging over the sinks, cascading ferns stashed on the
stoves. The refrigerators appeared to be Greek col-
umns, wound with paper roses. Portable floodlights
suddenly bathed the flowered cupboards and Mrs.
Butor in a hideous glare. She waved her scarf de-
murely. Good grief, it's a wedding. She's come up
with something worse than dancing. She's done it
again. Who made the refreshments? Where is the
groom?

"Now, gals. Today I present my LIFE." She
squinted at the lights and moved forward. "You perhaps did not know that I spent fifteen years studying
ballet with Taglionova." An awed "wow" followed
that revelation. Had everyone gone batty? "I shall
demonstrate the posture, the basic positions, and
some fundamental steps—*pas*." She minced backwards, going into a sort of foul-shot crouch. I
watched, transfixed with disbelief.

"Does she expect me—?"

"Of course I can't expect to teach *Swan Lake* to
ball players."

"We're not ball players," someone said primly.

"Well then, to girls of your age. One must begin
ballet in the cradle. One learns the *jeté* as one learns
to walk. But now that you've caught on to dancing
and seem to enjoy it—all but a few of you . . ." She
turned in my direction, but the smoke and glare
saved me from those accusing eyes. ". . . enjoying it
all, I thought we'd spend the next six weeks on modern dance. It's not exactly ballet, but . . ."

"Six weeks! Do you expect me—?"

"I've ordered your leotards. You can pick them up

in the dean's office after school. Take along five dollars."

"Leotards! Five dollars!"

"And never mind gym shoes. We'll dance barefooted. Isadora would love that. The simplicity, the harmonious simplicity of that."

"Do you expect me to wear a leotard and skip among these doilies? I will not dance. I will not dance." I rocketed from the room.

When I reached the gym I found Coach O'Hara in his office. He'd come in to grab a stopwatch for timing wind sprints. Right from the start this football season, his team had led the Northern Virginia League, as usual, and they weren't about to slip out of that position if he could help it. Not this year or ever. As always, he frightened me: those large teeth, the square jaw, the ruthless brown eyes behind thick, tinted glasses, a kelly-green baseball cap hiding the last of the great crew cuts. He didn't mess around.

I sat down, trying to look helpless. I cleared my throat twice. Everything about him, including the meticulous office with its wall-to-wall football trophies and framed mottos, told me to shut up. "Pressure Makes the Man," I read, and "Second Place Is Second Rate," and "Might Makes Right—in Football," and "Adversity Brings Forth the Blessings of Heaven." This man would never plead, "Win one for the Gipper."

"You'd better not hang around this gym," he said, getting ready to leave. "You'll fall through to China."

I looked out at Hiroshima, by now a quiet chasm, not a workman in sight.

"Gone for the day. Friday, you know. And I've got to get back to football practice. Why aren't you in class?"

I looked him squarely in the eye, and took a breath.

"I won't dance. I won't dance another dance." I looked away.

"Well, you are really something, you are," he said, shaking his head.

"I won't dance. I won't go back there. I'll never set foot in a home ec room again."

"Tell that to Mrs. Butor," he said, opening a locker and handing me a Baby Ruth. "For dancing energy." He glared hard at me.

"I will have my feet amputated before I go back to that icky dance hall. Here, I don't need your energy." He stood directly in front of me, jaw jutting menacingly. He took the candy bar and looked down at me.

"Your task is to dance. Mine is to go back to practice." He left the office, striding toward the field. I followed.

"I will cut off my arms and legs rather than wear a leotard." He gained on me. "I'll have myself committed to the state mental hospital, where everyone else around here belongs. I will not simper under paper pansies when I belong in *there*." I pointed to the gym. Coach blew his whistle at the beef trust, his linemen. I stopped and watched. "Or . . . out . . . here!" I pointed to the field.

"Pulling guards and tackles, get ready for sprints. Today it's forty yards in under six seconds or head for the showers. On your mark."

"Or out here, Coach. Couldn't I come out here, Coach, and work out with your team? Exercise? You know, train?"

"Get set . . ."

"I can run as fast as these guys, Coach, and catch and throw."

"Go!" The beef trust broke off the starting line and across the grass while Coach watched the second hand sweep along. "Run, boys, run! And you, go inside and dance. Run, run!"

"I wouldn't get in your way, Coach. I'd carry out the equipment and help you." The linemen were by now coming back to check their times, Coach yelling their errors as they approached. I looked around the field for an ally. I looked further and further. Across the street the lacrosse field stood empty except for a man cutting the grass.

"Where's the J.V.?" I wondered aloud, remembering that the only boys I knew played on the junior varsity—the Baby Generals. Then I realized that the J.V.'s season had ended last week with the B.C.C. game. They usually scheduled only four games.

"You ran like a bunch of old spinsters out there, boys. Let's go again."

"Coach, how about the lacrosse field?"

"We'll never beat G.W. with these times!"

"How about letting me have the lacrosse field? Me and the rest of our dance class. We need to exercise to keep in shape for the softball season."

"Take your mark again, boys."

"We wouldn't bother you. We'd just go across the street and play alone. You'd hardly even see us."

"Get set."

I took three steps and added myself to the lineup. I'd show him.

"Go!"

I broke out ahead of those lumbering linemen and ran the forty yards with hardly a gulp of air, finishing several strides ahead of the fastest offensive guard. I trotted back to the stopwatcher.

"Well, that's what dancing will do for you every time," said Coach O'Hara. "You can have the lacrosse field, and I'll even throw in a ball."

Chapter 6

Slog. We got a slog ball. I hadn't seen one since second grade. Now it reminded us that, yes, after all, we were only little girls fooling around with a red rubber ball—bubble-gum red at that. A sort of beach ball washed up from our past. About the size of a rugby ball, but much lighter, it bounced hugely in our efforts to drop kick, pass, toss, dribble, hit and belt it. "It's probably trying to remind us that we should be in dancing class," I ventured to the small gathering. "So let's play slog for starters, just to get our wind back." We were off.

I had spent the weekend on the phone snatching dancers from the brink of Isadoraville. Surprising how few of my old volleyball mates wanted to join us on the boys' lacrosse field. Only E.J. came along without a struggle. "How did you do it?" she asked. "And why not sooner? Exactly what did you say to Coach O'Hara to make him give up his precious field?"

"I cried a lot. Besides, he's not all that generous. This field wouldn't have been used until spring."

Then Teeny came along too, although she tried to give us a little static. "Just when I was learning to operate the phonograph!"

"Yes, but Aileen was moving in on you. She's been taking private lessons in the A-V center." After three calls, Putt joined us, and Joan Sterne and Polly Miller, Teeny's twin. I tried Natalie next.

"No. I'm not leaving the comfort of the kitchen," she said. "Have you forgotten it's October. The rains should be along any day now. You'll come back to the stoves."

"I promise there will be no rain. I give you my word," I heard myself saying.

"Okay, if you say so. But on cold days I'm taking a sick cut."

By now Rinehart also manned the phones. He called the dancers' brothers to ask them to intercede. He vowed his help in all science courses. He pledged to help one girl win the American Legion Oratorical Contest and to another offered his services for forging absentee excuses. I overheard him even promise to tutor a victim for a parts-of-speech makeup exam. He stopped at nothing. He's completely unscrupulous. But he got me Phyllis and Millie Murphy and he almost delivered Aileen, the beauty. Finally I called her and alternately threatened, cajoled, nagged, bullied, implored, and wheedled her. She had apparently fallen in love with her leotard.

"You can wear it on the field," I said, knowing she'd soon have to cover it with a rain parka or at least a slicker. "Plus, the football team practices near our new field. The boys come out during last period and do exercises. They'll have time to watch you in your pink tights." I would have promised her refreshments and a groom.

"But what about the dirt? I'll soil my new costume."

"Aileen, the rest of us will be the dirtballs. All you have to do is to stand around and root for us. You're our gorgeous cheerleader." I knew that if she came, her clique would eventually come too, and we needed more bodies. So now we had ten for slog that first day and eleven by Wednesday—Bumpy Bumstead. Word had gotten around that the football team cheered our efforts. They didn't.

But Mrs. Butor did. She was glad to get rid of the lot of us. "More dancing room for the truly talented," she told our spy, Charlotte, who hung in there at the cooking-room cotillions. We all knew that Coach O'Hara could handle the fat one.

"Coach will ply Butor with cookies," said Rinehart, with perfect fat-power logic.

"She's afraid of him, just like everyone else is—except me," I fibbed.

Even my mom relished the ball game. "Now you'll stop complaining about that woman and your two left feet," she told me, "and your father won't have to buy you another gym uniform. You'd be hard on leotards, I'm afraid."

Back to slog. Remember it? Everyone lines up in baseball positions. One team fields, another "bats," except the pitcher rolls the rubber ball to the plate and the "batter" kicks it, running to first base while the fielders retrieve the ball. A dumb game, really, but we played with good cheer. I captained the Blues, E.J. the Grays, Aileen cheered coquettishly. I decided to borrow a pair of cleats with a heavy kicking toe. I wanted to boom a homer over into the football field. Coach could field it. But then Wednesday we switched to soccer. E.J. had learned it at camp, so she taught us the fundamentals.

"All right, let's get the ball rolling. The flick pass, usually made while dribbling." E.J. showed us a short deceptive kick to a teammate. "The clearing kick." She sent the ball bounding forty yards. "Now heeling, a backward pass made with the heel of the foot. It's tricky." Slim and swift, her solemn green eyes darting around to make sure everyone watched, she demonstrated each play and position like a pro. "Center forward, you're the key," she said, taking Teeny aside for some special passing practice. They ran through their plays without the ball. We kept it and lined up to practice dribbling, not to be confused with bouncing the basketball by hand. Up and down the field we ran, controlling the ball with little taps of the feet, occasionally sending a long-distance boomer to the lacrosse goals. Some of the Catholic kids had learned to play in their elementary school. Their skills came back readily. Even with the wrong ball, our too-light high bouncer, we played well for our age. I played with relish, but not much style. It seemed strange to let your hands just dangle and flop by your side, good for nothing but keeping balance. Too bad we couldn't throw.

By our next session E.J. had scrounged some more balls. Now spheres of all sizes and colors flew through "heading" practice. We learned to use the flat center part of the forehead to propel a ball intercepted in mid-air.

"Great fun—exhilarating," cried E.J. from her position as wing, where her speed and footwork quickly made her our high scorer. She moved down the sidelines like a finely trained distance runner, unruffled by the defense. Putt played fullback and Millie halfback. They posed no threat to the fluid E.J. For my part, I chose goalie. Here my inexperienced footwork would be noticed least. I could use my hands—the only player with that privilege.

"Kick it through me," I'd urge, and lunge out for a save. "Kick it by me. Kick it over me. Kick it at me. Come on. Come on." Life could get pretty pushy around the net.

The weather held. The field, crisp and dry as

Astroturf, became our afterschool haven as well as our deliverance from the dance floor. Some days we played until 5:00 P.M. Rinehart usually came to the cage to watch my progress.

"You look like a scruffy blonde lepidopterist catching butterflies in a huge net," he said.

"Let me be a simple athlete catching balls, kicking balls. That's best."

"Not to a man of science."

"Watch me save a goal." I dived for one of E.J.'s half-volley kicks.

"I guess you mean well." Rinehart's favorite dump on someone. "Oh, he means well," he'd say when Mr. Manfred mispronounced a word on the loudspeaker. "She means well," he'd say when Miss Harrison told us that her favorite book in college was *Crime and Prejudice* by Jane Austen. "I wonder if she also liked *Pride and Punishment?* She means well."

"Watch me kick this fifty yards," I yelled at Rinehart.

"I'm going before the animals get here." He meant the football players. They now came regularly after their own practice to give us the benefit of their smart mouths. They'd lie about, shouting directions, orders, and abuse. Rinehart hated them as much as I did. But today he stayed.

"Our day will come, you creep fink," I finally hollered, when a pipsqueak from the second string ran out into the penalty area to advise me to kick for the corners. "Our day will come." It would, too.

And it started to come that very instant. Now Coach O'Hara, calling his troops to head for the showers and leave the girls alone, stopped by my net to ask if we were learning.

"Yes, sir, considering you gave us a slog ball." He seemed less terrifying than last time we'd met. He took off his cap. He ran his tanned hands over his crew cut. He watched me. Under his gaze I muffed a few.

"You're catching with your wrists. Get your fingers out first, ahead of your wrists. Here. Let me show you."

I threw him a pale blue and silver dodge ball, one of our many blimps.

"Don't let it sail away."

"How can you catch this child's ball?" he said. "One good belt and it's back in the dime store." But we flipped it around a few minutes. He was right. I'd been lazy about catching. I set out to improve.

"This ball's for water polo. Let me get you another." He rounded up the remaining boys, trooping with them toward the locker room.

Shadows fell on the field as we gathered up our soccer balls and started for the cinder track. One final circle before going home. I was lapping the others and heading for the stretch when Buddy, Coach's team manager, waved at me from the finish line.

"Hey, Zan, Coach said to give you this," he called, tossing me a football. "He says you'll know what to do with it. Have a ball."

Chapter 7

What a ball of fire our team turned into now! We named ourselves the Catch-11's and swore we'd learn how to control that goofy inflated oval. We discovered right off that a football zigs and zags unpredictably when kicked or thrown. It squibbles away just when you think you have a good hold.

"Teeny, it's only a bladder covered with leather," I said after she had dropped it thirteen times in a row. She snuffled. "You'll soon find the handle," I told her. "Don't give up."

"But what part is played by these ratty laces? Am I supposed to catch it by these?" She held up the mangy old ball that Coach had lent us. Its laces drooped from her hand.

"Here, let me fix that," said Rinehart. He had skipped study hall to attend our first football session. He watched with great glee . . . then wrath . . . then growing alarm as we muffed every punt, pass, and place kick. He tied the laces fast and then took out a little pocketknife he always carried to dissect insects. He cut off the frayed ends. "There. Now, get your fingers out first, ahead of your wrists. Grab hold and bring the ball into your chest. Hang on to it. And don't give up." Then he backed away and threw Teeny the ball, a weak, underhand pass that hit her shins. I watched as Teeny tossed it back to him. He held his hands up to his face, making no attempt to catch it as it caromed off his ear. Thud. His poor, frail head.

"Rinehart, you stole that catching advice from Coach O'Hara," I said.

"Of course I did. And all of you need it—and a lot more."

"But you can't even throw or catch. You can't practice what you preach."

"So what? I can preach while you practice. And I will. A lot."

Most of the kids on our team had never handled a football. I was the most experienced. I'd thrown the ball around every fall with my brother, Homer, before he joined the Midget League and dropped me as a receiver. I'd gotten used to its weird shape. I could pass fairly well—long bloopers that wobbled but got there. I'd been to every game our boys had played over the last two years. I had learned a lot from them. Millie had learned to catch from her older brother, who used her as a target every fall on his way to making All-American. She was accustomed to catching zippy, stingy passes, but quickly adjusted and learned to haul in my floaters. E.J. had played football at camp—with the cook and his kitchen helpers after dinner—until a counselor discovered she was skipping the marshmallow roasts to learn "a boy's sport." E.J. remembered some formations and plays and could kick soccer-style field goals. Her speed would come in handy in the backfield.

Of our other players, only Aileen had touched a football. Her boyfriend played center at St. Vincent's Prep and practiced a few snaps to her on the beach every summer. On Sunday afternoons Nat and Phyllis watched pro games on TV with their fathers. They could each name three quarterbacks—the same three.

They remembered a few picturesque terms like "suicide squad," "statue-of-liberty play," and "bungle"—they meant "fumble"—but they didn't know the meanings. They did recall the colors of the Kansas City Chiefs. Yes, they seemed ready for some heavy action on the line. But they had never even touched a football before that day.

So there we were, ready for Rinehart's advice. He didn't fail us. That first session he ran us through a kind of practice he'd read about in a novel.

"*Tiny Sonny*." he said. "It's not by Hesse. Only sports novel I ever chose for a book report. Had to in sixth grade. *Tiny Sonny, Ace Quarterback*. Sonny's team drilled on pass patterns for three whole chapters. Let's do that, since it's all I can remember about football." Rinehart explained some simple terms like "passer," "receiver," "downfield," "sideline catch," "screen pass," and "cut." Then we all lined up to practice. Teeny stopped crying.

I got in line to run out for the ball. But who's going to throw it?

"All right now, Zanzibar, you're my ace quarterback—'Tiny Sonny.' Stand here and throw the ball to these receivers. They're each to run a screen pattern." I started lobbing my bombs to them. He watched a round or two, making impatient sounds with his cracking knuckles. "We need to speed things up. Keep at it."

With that, Rinehart took off for the boys' practice field. The guy can run, I thought as I watched him snatch two footballs from the ball bag and head back to our turf.

In the next hour, E.J. and I threw a zillion passes. Our teammates began to catch with skill. "Get your fingers out there, not your wrists," Rinehart kept

yelling. "Hang on to it! Grab it! Grab it!" He taught
us the post pattern, a pass route where a receiver runs
downfield, then cuts diagonally towards the goal
posts. Since we had no goal posts, we ran it into the
lacrosse nets. Millie took to that one right away. She
used her size to ram the net. Occasionally E.J. joined
the pass receivers. Rinehart decided that her speed
would be best for the fly pattern, so he taught it to
us. "You simply fly down the field at top speed," he
explained. "Fly—and don't forget to catch the pass."
Aileen liked the screen play best because she had to
run only a few yards, thus keeping her leotard
"fresh." The rest of us wore sweaters and jeans by
now, but she hadn't noticed.

Before we quit for the day, Rinehart tramped his
Catch-11's across the street. He wanted us to learn the
layout of a real football field. He asked Coach O'Hara,
busy with his own late practice, to point out the key
positions.

"Not today. I'm working with the defense. But my
quarterback is loafing," Coach added, pointing to
Randy Boyle lying on the bench. "He'll help you."

Coach adjusted his baseball cap and turned back to
the beef trust. Rinehart watched him jot a few notes
on a clipboard, then walked over to Randy.

"Oh, no I won't. I ain't helping these girls with
nothin'. They shouldn't be out here in the first place.
They're turning into jocks and ruining our lacrosse
field. It won't be fit for spring season after they finish
groveling all over it. The grass is dying. They're breaking down the nets."

"We are not," muttered Millie.

"Get back in there where you belong. You misfits,
you freaks!" He pointed and flailed his arm so strenu-
ously that he fell off the bench. He gestured from the

ground to the home economics wing. "The field's our style, the boys' sod. That's your style, up there where you should be." Someone shook a dustmop from a third-floor window in reply.

"Randy, you're a loathsome rodent," said Rinehart, and motioned us to leave. But Buddy, the bantamweight manager, caught up with our disheartened footballers.

"I'll show you the field. Don't let Randy get you down. He thinks he's a superstar after the Williamsburg game."

With that, Buddy taught us about yard lines, side lines, goal lines, and the end zone. Rinehart listened intently, asking his usual pushy questions. Buddy didn't seem to mind and ended with a stirring speech about goal-line stands. "You can say all you want about offense, but a tough defense wins championships," he concluded. "Look at Coach there. He gives more time to the defense than to his offensive backfield. He knows the score." Rinehart had long since taken out the notebook he carried for homework assignments. He wrote rapidly, underlining and circling certain phrases.

"Football is really quite scientific," he announced on the way home that day. He had been silent for ten minutes. Now a few more "hmmms" as we approached the county library and then, "I'll see you in English. I plan to get out of study hall more—maybe for good. I'll tell my Dad I need the time to perfect my biology project." He made for the card catalog.

"You should escape your Tuesday-Thursday study hall, too, Zan," said E.J. on the phone that night. "Then you could practice every day."

"I bet some of the rest of you could juggle your schedules so we could work out as a team—practice together every day."

"I know I can. My counselor's a pushover."

"See ya."

"See ya tomorrow."

I went to sleep dreaming of the perfect pass spiraling toward two outstretched arms. The crowd roared. "Thatagirl, Zan. Way to zing 'em in there, Zanballer."

When Rinehart appeared next morning for second period, he was swinging an unfamiliar attaché case. "Borrowed it from my dad," he whispered, producing a key and snapping the lock. He pulled out a mound of mimeographed papers. His purply fingers told me that he'd been down in his basement pressroom, knocking out the monthly *Rinehart's Science Newsletter*.

"You're all gooey, Rinehart. Here, I don't want to read about your dumb turbo engines." I pushed away the stuff he tried to hand me.

"Wrong again, rookie. I have here in my hand your playbook for football practice." His eyes crinkled in a grin. Even his glasses had blotches of ink on them.

I took the smudgy sheets and started to look them over, while Fuzzy droned on about the interjection. Our class had finally made it to my favorite part of speech. At the rate we were going we might run out of parts by spring. What would she teach then, I wondered.

"What's a playbook?" I wrote in my notes, shoving them over so Rinehart could read.

"A compilation of offensive and defensive plays and maneuvers; a listing of each football player's position and moves on each play," he wrote back.

Eight stapled pages! He must have been up all night. The cover read "PROPERTY OF CATCH-11. REWARD FOR RETURNING," and under that, "Compiled and Published by Coach Arthur Rinehart." A small drawing of a football with thick laces completed the cover.

"Where did you get this stuff?" I scribbled, pretending to be copying the interjections that Fuzzy now listed on the board.

"In novels—where else?" he whispered. "Good old fiction I got at the library. I read the entire *Tiny Sonny* series last night. Football's about a lot more than just throwing and catching. Old swivelhips Sonny turns into a fleet runner in Volume II, a supreme kicker in Volume III, a gutsy fullback in Volume IV . . ."

"And let me guess—a defensive specialist in Volume V?"

"Yes, a middle-linebacker."

I slid the playbook into my ringbinder and opened it. On the first page burst forth Rinehart's line drawing of a football field. He'd used the three-dimensional style he'd developed for illustrating his *Science Newsletter*.

I studied the drawing. We'd covered that yesterday, thanks to Buddy. I turned the page to a glossary of terms. A few of these we had learned, but most were new to me. What could "intentional grounding" mean? "Play action pass"? "Red dog"? I skipped over and looked at a bunch of stick figures in a circle: "Huddle." I flipped through "Rules and Game Progress." "Skills and Fundamentals," and "Formations and Strategy" before coming on a little paragraph called "Equipment and Uniforms." I wrote, "What's the point of this? We'll never get uniforms. We're oh so lucky to have three broken-down footballs."

Rinehart frowned as he wrote. "Remember O'Hara's law: 'Adversity Brings Forth the Blessings of Heaven'? I'm now unveiling Rinehart's Law: 'Be Kind to Buddy.' "

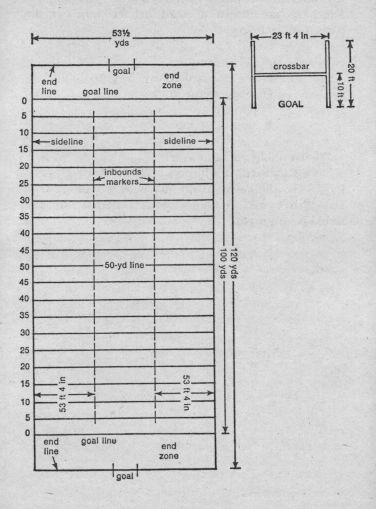

I read about pads, cleats, helmets, jerseys, tape. Rinehart had drawn a small helmet, labeling the parts in a key below.

A. Chin Strap
B. Face Guard (Heavy Wire)
C. Suspension Strap
D. Crown
E. Ear Covering

What a nubby thing to wear!

"Say, Rinehart," I whispered. "How about Hagen's Law?" On the cover of my playbook I wrote, "Our Day Will Come." I didn't know then that our day would be our *night*.

Chapter 8

Journal Entry # 1

I've always believed that girls who keep diaries must be loony boobs. "DEAR DIARY!!!!!! WOW!!!!! HE LOOKED AT ME TODAY IN MATH!!!!!! I LOVE HIM!!!!!! DOES HE LOVE ME???????????? WOW!!!!! I HOPE SO!!!!!!!" Feh. Ugh. Only a dolt would carry on that way. But Rinehart convinced me yesterday to keep track of our football progress in an orderly way. He bought me this red ledger with money from his *Newsletter* budget. He says that all writers keep journals and that more and more athletes are becoming writers after they retire. He borrowed six autobiographies by football players for me to read. He says he'll ghostwrite my autobiography if I ever need him. But how can I become an ex-basketball player if I never get to play? I'll have to retire from football. First I must learn the game.

Today we began practice with a bunch of warm-up exercises that Rinehart copied from the boys' team. He showed us arm swings, cross-body double arm circles, waist bends and rotations, side-leg kicks, toe pushups, knee pushups, and then we did a lot of toe-heel prancing. They're all harder than jumping jacks. Then I threw passes from a formation we're learning. E.J. practiced field goals. She sailed a few over the lacrosse net from thirty yards away. Polly holds for her. After practice I checked out the gym. Footings have been poured. I left messages in the wet cement. "Work faster, you stiffs" was the only nice one.

Journal Entry # 2

Rinehart came out with a clipboard and stopwatch. He's not saying where he got them. We exercised. His coordination improves every day, but his glasses fall off a lot. He says he needs them in order to watch us. He counts every motion. The tight T formation seems pretty easy. Rinehart thinks I'll have to become a scrambler. He says I'm not tall enough to be a drop-back passer because I won't be able to see my receivers over my linemen. Aileen can snap the ball now. She asked her boyfriend to teach her. She's figured out that the center runs less than other players. "It's even easier than dancing," E.J. heard her say in the bathroom.

Entry # 3

After exercising we drilled on pass patterns out of the tight T. Buddy gave Rinehart an ear-splitting silver whistle. Looks like E.J. will be a halfback. Positions so far:

THE TIGHT T

Rinehart timed Polly with his new stopwatch (he said he was giving up cupcakes for lunch and had sold a few old science projects) and feels she is perfect for the left halfback. Millie might be switched to tight end if we learn other formations.

Entry # 4

Saturday night. Played football since 10:00 A.M. The boys never work out on game day so our backfield made itself at home on their turf. Our linemen couldn't come since most of them were going to the boys' game at Swanson. Rinehart filled in at center. He's not as good as Aileen. E.J. practiced kicking off to us. Buddy gave her a kicking tee so she can really wham them. I ran back about fifty kickoffs. I'm exhausted, but it sure is great to cross that goal line. Touchdowns count more than baskets, too!

Entry # 5

I read autobiographies all morning because it's raining too hard to go out and run windsprints. Football players have terrific nicknames. Like Bulldog, Doc, Turk, Crazy Legs, Bobo, Mr. Outside, Hopalong, Golden Boy, Phantom, Mighty Moe, the Doaker, Zipper Head, Whizzer. I think I'll become the Zammer. I hung an old tire in the garage and passed for the hole. Easy enough when the tire stands still. Harder when it swings. Tomorrow before school will move tire to backyard so I can stand back farther. Must develop long-distance accuracy. E.J. called and we tested each other on the playbook. Her leg is stumpy and stiff from kicking. She plans to ask Buddy for a football shoe—maybe two.

Entry # 6

It rained again today. We stayed in study hall and memorized the new plays that Rinehart added to our books. Charlotte Cardenez and JoJo Rice asked to join Catch-11. They loathe modern dance. JoJo's a blimp and can't find a leotard to fit. Hooray!! We now have two substitutes.

Entry # 7

Rain. Our field's a lagoon. We went over to exercise in Rinehart's basement. Did one hundred squat jumps and stomach rocks. Also mastered the scissors kick. Rinehart told me to carry a football around *at all times*. That way I won't ever fumble, he says. He read that trick in *A Boy's Book of Beginning Ball*. He's reading non-fiction now! I fooled around with his chemistry set and looked at his butterfly collection.

Entry # 8

If it doesn't stop raining I'll go as crazy as Mrs. Butor. We picked up another refugee from her kitchen today. We should change the team's name to Fourteen Footballers, or some such.

Entry # 9

Finally. All clear. But cold and muddy. To practice I wore Homer's letter sweater from the Little League. Where does he keep his helmet? Began with flutter kicks and leg lifts. Then we broke into three groups. E.J. punted one of the balls to Polly for run backs. Rinehart used another ball to work the defense on recovering fumbles. He fumbled. They recovered. He fumbled about a thousand times. He's a pro at it. With our third ball I practiced laterals to my full-back, Millie. When she got used to the backward pass, as she calls the lateral, we worked on hand-offs. I'd take the snap, swing right or left, and hand her the ball as she charged by. Rinehart's got her on a special diet of malted milks to "build her up even more." We played till dark. My head is muddy but unbowed.

Entry # 10

A strange thing happened today in the cafeteria. Mr. Manfred stopped me as I was going through the lunch line and asked why I was carrying a football under my left arm. Couldn't think of what to answer. Heard myself muttering, "Taking it to my boyfriend." Right away he smiled like when he told me about the spelling bee. He said I looked "healthier" and "even prettier" since I started my dancing class. I almost dropped my tray, so I faked to the left, spun around, and handed it off to him. He congratulated me on my footwork. He said, "I hope to see you again soon, Isadora. Heh Heh. You're becoming more feminine. You may get Lee High into the newspapers yet!" He must not have noticed my warm-up jacket. Doesn't he know what's going on in his own school? Say, what was he doing out of his office anyway?

I practiced scrambling today and throwing to the opposite direction from the way I ran. My arm's beginning to feel like a zip gun.

Entry # 11

The quarterback sneak. What a play! I take the ball from center and move straight ahead, trying to get between the defenders. Also love the bootleg!! In this one I take the snap, fake a handoff to the fullback or halfbacks, hide the ball on my hip, and then sweep around end. I stiff-arm all the guys in my way. Rinehart wore a green sun visor to practice, although we haven't seen that dying star all week. Fuzzy finally took R.'s exam off her bulletin board. It was all yellow and faded. The edges curl where she wrote "Arthur—a stupendous achievement—A+." Must begin fixing up my Globe Theater. The science fair begins in a few weeks. Rinehart's project remains a secret, even from me.

Entry # 12

Our players come out daily now. On cold weekends, too. We used the boys' field again. Grueling workout. Rinehart's a slave driver. Exercise. Grass drills!! "Lift your legs up off the grass. Now down. Face the grass. Now up. Run in place. Run. Now down. Put your face in the grass and push. Up. Up. Down. Up." Then short yardage plays, punt returns, kickoff returns. Teeny blocked one of E.J.'s field goal attempts. We're all going to sit together at tonight's game to discuss formations and plays after each down.

Entry # 13

Lee's jumbo linemen held Swanson High to twenty yards rushing. A slaughterhouse down on the field. Créep Randy threw for a T.D. and ran for another. Afterwards E.J. and I went to Rinehart's basement for a skull session. Decided to change to the Generals' basic offensive formation.

THE SPLIT T

This afternoon R. came by to see me throw at the tire. He changed my stance, then moved me back farther and farther in case we ever need to use the shotgun formation. Now I can jump while throwing, throw off either foot as I sprint right or left, back pedal while throwing, and evade an onrushing lineman (Rinehart) while scrambling in any direction. I can still lob the ball but mostly zap it for speed. Rinehart timed me for a quick release. He gives me three seconds to find a receiver—the tire hole, fence post, tree trunk, or garage door knob. I wore Homer's helmet. He's gone hunting with Dad. When they get home Dad will catch my passes for an hour. He promised.

Entry # 14

Coach O'Hara watched us practice today!!!! I didn't know he was there until Rinehart warned me in a huddle. (Rinehart calls all our plays.) I looked over and saw Coach writing on his clipboard. I messed up a signal, fumbled, recovered, got stopped at the line of scrimmage then pushed back ten yards by onrushing Bumpy. She can really hurt a guy. We ran the same play four or five times again. I kept wondering what Coach wanted. Finally he swooped down on our huddle and told us that since his own team didn't practice anymore on Mondays after their Saturday games, he'd come out to see our progress. He then worked us until 7:00 P.M. At dusk we couldn't see the ball in flight. Our receivers complained that they were being beaned. So he moved us to the boys' field and turned on the lights!!!!! He gave R. his key. Told him to go in for the shoulder pads so we could block harder. They didn't fit, but our defense improved anyway. I'm learning when to eat the ball. Coach O'Hara kept yelling, "There's no place on the field for fumblers, bumblers, stumblers," and, "This is a game of abandon. Run. Run. Run." He told me I was out of my mind to think I could win with a pass play each time. Win what?????? Just when we'd be downcast after a blown play he'd shout, "Way to go, that's a good try. Way to hit." His lungs are strong. When Coach finally dismissed us, he gave Rinehart his notes and said, "Remember, the harder you practice the harder it is to surrender during a game." What game????????????

Entry # 15

Every period today Manfred announced that the Generals have been invited to the Dogwood Bowl, Virginia's top honor for high-school footballers. Seven times he interrupted our classes and said, "You all must attend to cheer your outstanding team and its all-State candidate, Randy Boyle." Ech. Rinehart drilled us on the blitz, something he learned from a book O'Hara lent him. It's a surprise defensive maneuver where one or more of the defensive backfield players charge across the line of scrimmage to toss me down before I get the pass away. Sometimes it's called "red dogging." Great word! Tonight I ache all over my body.

Entry # 16

Dear Diary: We held our final football practice today!!!!!!

Chapter 9

Scientifica Rineharticulum
Daily Log of Arthur Rinehart,
Volume VII, p. 58.

November 27, 9:47 P.M.

My scientific experiments and observations proceeded naturally until today. Unfortunately they will now remain incomplete and thus useless as a science project for the fair. Unless, of course, I am allowed to submit my study, "An Analysis of Girls' Muscular Structure, Strength, Speed, and Stamina when Compared to Certain Boys of Similar Ages," as a work in progress. Would an unfinished project win first prize? I doubt it.

I shall record the disruptive incident, Randy's dastardly tackle, in some detail. Because of him and his craven buddies, Catch-11 will never play football again. Here's what happened this afternoon.

At my daily football observation this afternoon I continued to measure the endurance of each player. Zanner ran a few stellar off-tackle plays. Her cleats are too big. If she could borrow a pair the right size she'd be the fastest subject in both my experimental and control groups. E.J.'s pass patterns have reached perfection. Even when she's double-teamed, those quick hands of hers get up for the ball and hang on when she comes down in traffic. Millie Murphy's weight gain had hardened into muscular tissue. She could knock over the goal posts. My incomplete statistics for all these subjects will prove astonishing to the editors of *American Coaches Quarterly,* where I plan to publish my findings.

To continue: At exactly 4:30 P.M. today we began to scrimmage. Offensive backfield v. defensive line. At 4:45 P.M. Randy Boyle and his backfield clan came to our field and started jeering at my team: "Weirdos, retards, wild women," *et al.* He waved at me and shouted "Hey, girlie." On the eighth play after their arrival, Zanner took the hike and looked for her receivers. When she saw they were all covered she decided not to risk an interception. She scrambled like a demon out of the pocket. (Science has no word for the finesse she shows under pressure.) She settled on a play-action run. She swept right end, broke away, and was going for the goal line when suddenly Rat Randy darted over from the sideline and tackled her. What a brutal jolt it was that sent both of them flying into the cage! He stood up and yelled, "Freak, psycho nut," and some other words that I will not record in a scientific work.

Zanner lay there a long time. Randy kept dashing around the cage chanting "Two, four, six, eight. See the freak no boy would date."

I ran over to pick Z. up. By then our entire team had gathered to help. But she got up on her own. One shoe was torn off. She limped badly and seemed to be bleeding from the nose—or mouth. Couldn't tell. She did not cry. She hung on to the net for three minutes. I asked Randy to go away, to leave us alone so we could practice. He laughed.

"What for?" he mocked. "Practice for what?" He hailed his gang and they left, hooting abuse. "You're nothing but a bunch of oddballs."

"Randy's vicious, but he's right," said Aileen. "What are we practicing for?"

"To learn football," said Teeny.

"To get better," E.J. threw in.

"To improve your coordination, your speed, stamina . . ." I volunteered.

"Why?" asked Aileen feebly.

"To win," Zan said. "So we can win."

"Win what?" everyone said at once. "To win what?"

November 28, 8:30 A.M.

For the sake of science and football I visited Coach O'Hara early this morning at his house. I arrived at 7:00 A.M. I found him eating breakfast and reading the sports page. I returned the books he had lent me. We chatted about trap plays. He suggested that my team work harder on the power sweep, his favorite bread-and-butter play. He gave me a bowl of wheat germ and molasses. What follows is an exact transcript of the rest of our conversation.

"Mr. O'Hara. Our plays. Our team. That's what I've come to see you about."

"How can I help you? With all that natural talent —some of the finest athletic ability I've encountered in all my years as coach—you shouldn't be needing much help."

"But I do need help. All but one member of my team has quit."

"That's ridiculous. Why would they want to stop practicing? They've come all this way. That team shapes up to a fine one, one that could beat—"

"Beat who? That's just it."

"They'll never go back to dance class, not now, not after trying something worthwhile. Football's more than a sport. It's both physical and intellectual. It's a way of life. They realize that now."

"But Coach, my team feels—"

"Besides, Mrs. Butor will soon be starting instruction in social dance. Zan couldn't stand the mambo for even one second. Say, can you imagine her waltzing in those big cleats? She'll be back."

"She hasn't left. She'll practice on, even with a swollen ankle and a split lip. She apparently has a high tolerance for pain. She'll play without the team, too."

"The others?"

"They feel . . . they believe that practice is useless because we won't be playing any games. That's what matters to them."

"Well, they really are something, they are. Skill matters. And style of play. And form. And staying in good health—keeping in shape. That counts. Personal satisfaction comes from self-improvement, *any* self-improvement. I won't have them quit. I won't hear any more about it. I hate quitters. Those girls cannot quit!"

"Mr. O'Hara, my team would rather samba than aim at a dead end. They will not come back without a game to work for."

"Okay, I'll get 'em a game."

"How? Where? When?"

"Well, they can play my third string. Yes, of course they can. For starters they can whip my own benchwarmers. A game will give them all something to do. Pass the word to your girls that they will scrimmage my third string the end of this week. That should do it. In the stadium after school."

November 28, 12:21 P.M.

I have passed the word. Catch-11 practices again this afternoon! Until dark. Now they have something to work for. Coach O'Hara will arrange to leave his own team during their drill (for the Dogwood Bowl next week) and come over to our field for some last-minute instructions. He told Buddy to give Zan some aspirin and tape her ankle before we start exercising.

November 28, 10:07 P.M.

Acting in my capacity of publicity director for Catch-11 I wrote, printed, and then delivered (by riding the bus) the following press release to every newspaper in the Washington area:

LOCAL GIRLS' FOOTBALL TEAM CHALLENGES
BOYS IN GAME OF THE CENTURY

Two football teams, each comprised of Robert E. Lee students, will face each other tomorrow at Lee Stadium (1947 Nellie Custis Boulevard at Old McLean Highway). The girls' team, Catch-11, is the first of its kind, certainly in the South and perhaps in the entire country as well. Catch-11 has been organized by Arthur Rinehart, the well-known blue ribbon winner for two consecutive years in Arlington County's Science Fair. (Scientists will perhaps remember his first prize for "Mold Cultures as Grown in Locker 888" and for his fantastic display of butterflies caught at Lubber Run Park.) Mr. Rinehart believes (and has believed for many years) that girls, if given the opportunity and encouragement, are able to develop the same strength, speed, stamina, and muscle structure as boys. His quarterback tomorrow will be Zan Hagen, who is coming off a severe injury sustained during an intrasquad scrimmage. Reporters attending will be seated on the fifty-yard line. Following the game, a press party to meet Catch-11 will be held at 17-14 Glebe Road, Arlington, Virginia—a short walk from the stadium.

November 28, 10:35 P.M.

Z. just called. She can't sleep. Too excited about the game. I told her to fall asleep immediately so she can remember the formations tomorrow. Why isn't she tired after that grueling practice?

We had only just finished our exercises today when O'Hara joined us. He came right to the point. Said we'd have to perfect our defense before he'd let us play, then knelt down by the bench and drew in the dirt the basic defensive formation.

Buddy gave out helmets—sort of busted-down ones, yet they are all ours for the game. Coach threw passes to me and Buddy for an hour while my defensive backfield batted them down. I didn't catch one. The

THE BASIC DEFENSIVE FORMATION

defensive line practiced rushing the passer. Zan tried out at right safety, then right cornerback. She has quick reflexes and is fast enough for either position, but finally settled for middle linebacker so she can call defensive plays. I'd like her to rest on the bench when Catch-11 is defending, but with only fourteen players she'll have to stay in the entire game.

Coach taught the front four to come off the snap quickly in order to pressure the quarterback into passing before the receivers are ready. He also taught them how to chase a runner along the line of scrimmage—"lateral pursuit" he called it. He made E.J. a free safety. Told her to roam the field, to shadow the ball, try to get a feel on each play just where the ball will be thrown—then get there first. He hollered at Millie, "Your size will be wasted unless you've mobility to go with it. Move. Move. Terrorize the passer." He explained how everyone had to be on guard against the quarterback sneak, the draw, and the end sweep—his team's basic ground gainers. In the dusty lacrosse cage he drew his three favorite pass patterns.

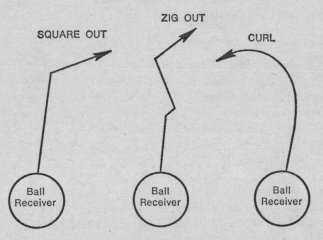

THREE PASS PATTERNS

"Watch especially for these, girls. My third-string quarterback doesn't have enough on the ball to throw long, so he uses these for short gainers." Coach criticized his own man! Randy's pal, Fritz—he led the "Weirdo" chant—will quarterback. I must not become emotionally involved. I must gather enough statistics and facts from the game to complete my science project. But we must win!

November 29, 12:15 P.M.

Z. went to the library to rest up. She ate a large breakfast, will skip lunch, then consume a cup of honey one hour before kickoff. I had to show her the very *Pro Football Digest* that recommends honey over chocolate for energy. Catch-11 suits up at 2:00—white sweatshirts with lavender satin numbers hand-stitched by Aileen. Jeans, tennis shoes, or cleats (if they can be borrowed), and helmets. I've given them the instructions that Coach O'Hara mimeographed for us. No tackling will be allowed. Every player must wear a red handkerchief in the right back pocket. Instead of tackling a ball carrier, the defender must grab the handkerchief and pull it out. Then the whistle blows the play dead. Each quarter will last five minutes, with Buddy keeping time and Coach being referee, umpire, head linesman, field judge, and back judge all at once. I've decided to let Zan call her own game so that I can be free to time each player and take the necessary notes for exact comparisons. I must keep my mind on the culmination of my experiment. Can we win? We must!!!

November 29, 1:00 P.M.

I turned in to Coach O'Hara my official lineup for today's game. I noticed his lineup included some of the same goofballs who almost made my team quit on Wednesday. Coach named them Captains because they're only third-string Generals. Very shortly they will become privates—when we finish with them.

November 29, 8:30 P.M.

In the name of Albert Einstein and in fairness to the hallowed tradition of biology/physics/chemistry, I, Arthur Rinehart, renounce my former claim to a scientists's title. A scientist should follow through on his task. He should get the facts. He must carry on with his work in the face of attempted opposition and diversion. He must be dispassionate. He must not be emotional. I have failed!

I am, however, still able to report the events leading to the above renunciation. As a final chapter in my nine-volume lifework, I shall reveal all.

The game today began in revolution and ended in ignominy. First of all, Coach O'Hara announced that he would not, as usual, flip a coin to decide which team would kick off, which receive. Instead he said the girls got to receive because they are girls. He shouted, "Ladies first," and blew his whistle to start the game. An angry cry went up from the Captains, who felt cheated. Their storm was nothing compared to the girls' protest.

"So we are girls, so what? We don't need any special breaks. We want to play by official game regulations," cried Joan.

"We can hold our own even under the regular

rules. Don't give us favors," about six of my team said at once.

"Don't make up easy ways for us, just because you think we're patsys. We don't want your charity," yelled Z., stamping her cleated shoes. I had stuffed the toes with sweat socks, but they still looked as if they might fall off on the first series of downs.

"Why, how sweet of Coach to consider us," purred Aileen.

The few spectators on the sidelines started booing O'Hara, so he flipped a quarter to end the bedlam.

"Heads," said Zan.

"Tails it is."

"We'll receive," said Fritz. "You should have kept your freaky mouth shut."

They received, all right, and some blubbery boy waddled E.J.'s kickoff back about ten yards. First and ten, Captains.

The Captains, as third stringers, aren't exactly what you'd call picture-book players. Most of them are either overweight or undersized—definitely rejects. If I were Coach I wouldn't even let them warm my bench. But today Fritz had them riled up for the game. They made three first downs in a row before we stopped them on our own twenty-yard line. Fritz tried a field goal, but the ball looped off to the right. A bearded young guy I'd never seen before picked up the dead ball and tossed it back into the game. Then I watched him take a notebook from his pea jacket. He wrote something. Another scientist? Meanwhile I took notes of my own.

Z. called a quarterback draw that caught the Captains napping. Twenty quick yards. Then she handed off to Millie who found a big hole between the right defensive end and tackle. Ten more yards. Another first down. Then Z. zipped a pass to E.J., a beautiful delayed slant that worked for thirty yards. On the next play Polly fumbled but recovered for a small loss. I made a note to count errors by my players who had boyfriends watching. Might be a vital clue to performance. A sprinkling of onlookers stood around the field—maybe ten. Zan's mother smiled and waved. I recognized a few boyfriends and girls from the dancing class. They seemed to be shivering. All at once I felt cold, too. But what the heck, it's November. We've had all the breaks from the weather so far. As I counted the fans Polly dropped a pass. Then Fritz batted down a bullet in the end zone. Not to be outdone, he was playing defense as well as offense. A real smart aleck. So at fourth and twelve yards to go, Bumpy took my orders to E.J.—try for three points. E.J. kicked a field goal as the whistle shrilled, ending the quarter.

We had drawn first blood, and the Captains now roared to meet the kickoff. This time Fritz took the ball, broke away from the handkerchief grabbers, and sprinted sixty yards. He's certainly no passer, but he's a nimble creep. If I were Coach I'd move him to the defensive backfield. Zan finally caught him, snatching the handkerchief determinedly while dodging a wicked stiff-arm to the throat. But then, on the next play, Fritz handed off to his huge fullback who charged through the line scattering girls like pick-up sticks. He scored. Fritz kicked for the point after touchdown. Captains, 7; Catch-11, 3.

Nothing much happened the rest of that period. I took notes, timed all the pass patterns, sent in an occasional play, and watched the beard photographing my team. Why was he smiling? At the half, Referee O'Hara gave a five-minute break. We gathered for a pep talk. We felt we could take them. No one cried.

Buddy stuck tape on scratches and cleat marks. Numbers had been ripped off, blue jeans torn. I reminded Z. of our zig out, zig ins—trusty pass patterns. Everyone drank Gatorade and wondered where the crowds were. "No one heard about this game or the stadium would be full," I assured them.

"Coach should have announced it on the loudspeaker. Instead we got the Dogwood Bowl again all day," said Putt.

"It's just as well. I doubt if old Manfred would let us play if he knew. He hasn't even discovered our practice sessions. He thinks we're still up in the kitchen twinkle-toeing around the canisters."

"Good thing Aileen wears her leotard under her uniform. We're safe," said E.J., running back on the field to begin the second half.

I remember thinking that Zan's probably right about Manfred. I'd never met him. But still, wouldn't it be splendid to have thousands of fans cheering us on. Maybe I could rig a device to measure their sound and try to link the volume with successful plays. . . .

Z. took the kickoff, then got smeared at her own twenty. Some brute grabbed the handkerchief with one hand and shoved her down with the other. The referee ignored that move, but on the first play from scrimmage he blew his whistle, gave the sign for roughing the passer, and warned the boys against get-tough tactics. When the boys got the ball they marched quickly to our two. We held. Fritz decided not to take a chance. He kicked the shortest field goal in history. 10—3, Captains.

I stopped writing. I tossed my pen in the air. I flung down my clipboard and signaled for a time out. Zan came over to the bench. I told her we had to win, blast it. There could be no defeat for Catch-11. She agreed. I suggested we go for the long gainer. To heck with caution. My palms sweated. Good thing I didn't have to throw passes.

Aileen ran back the kickoff sixty yards. She seemed as surprised as her mates as she eluded four tubs of lard, a midget, a mastodon, and Fritz himself. She flitted across the chalk marks, falling out of bounds as a defender plunged at her.

Okay, now, this is it, I thought. And it was. Zan faded, then spied an opening in the line, scrambled toward it, then saw it close with a blob. She backpedaled, started forward again, headed for the sidelines, then saw Polly free in the end zone. She threw. The ball made a lazy arc, inching along like a Zeppelin, finally floating home to Polly's arms. She clung to it shouting, "Six points, six points." We had six more points.

We needed more. I paced the sidelines. I suffered a sudden attack of flopsweat. I let fly, drop kicking my notebook in an effort to help E.J. make that extra point. Catch-11 huddled, then broke out for the line. As they started positioning themselves for the conversion I suddenly saw a little bald fellow running toward the referee. He appeared to be choking for air. I screamed, "Ref, it's too late for a substitute on this play. He's too old. He can't come . . ." I saw that the guy wore a blue business suit. His tie must be gagging him. "He's a grown man—he can't play for—"

"Ladies, stop this at once," the suit bellowed.

Zan began to call signals. "Thirty-five, forty-one, fifty-two."

"Stop this immediately," the old guy bellowed again. "Do you hear me?"

"Hut one. Hut two."

"Ladies, ladies. You will cease or I'll—"

"Hut. Hut." Aileen snapped the ball, Zan twisted the laces away from E.J.'s foot, and the pigskin soared right between the goalposts. We had another point. Hot Ziggity.

"Young ladies, you will clear this field."

Something clicked in my mind as I noticed Baldy's brown shoes and white socks. Of course! He fitted Zan's description. The principal!

I lost my head completely. I ran onto the field. "Keep playing," I urged. "Line up again for the kickoff. We still have time. We can win." No one heard me. They watched Manfred. Livid with rage, he snatched O'Hara's whistle. His eyes bunged out as he blew a long blast.

"This disgrace—this football game—is over. Michael O'Hara, follow me to my office. You others, go home and bathe."

Coach trailed Manfred toward the building. Catch-11 left the field to a boys' chorus of "Guess we showed you, weirdos, freaks—girls!"

Showed us what? Exactly nothing. We played to a tie. In another minute we would have vanquished them.

Chapter 10

Rinehart's party for the press? For the first hour I thought it might be a total bust. Catch-11 met in Rinehart's basement after the game. While we relived each play of our "moral victory," Rinehart ran up to the kitchen and down to his dissecting table with plates of Bit O' Honey bars, pots of waxy honey, and pitchers of Tang. Rinehart's idea of refreshments —less refreshing, more energy. He even threw in twelve Hydrox cookies left over from his former belief in chocolate. We munched them and waited for reporters. We waited forty minutes. I began to feel my ankle throbbing again. I detected some new aches in my hips and thighs. Those Captain linemen had gotten in clouts when O'Hara hadn't been looking. The aspirin must be wearing off. I limped around the table, trying to shake out the stiffness in my knees.

"I got to go home, Rinehart. I hurt."

"Eat more, Zanner. Do knee bends. Totter up and down the steps. Jog into the furnace room. Don't think about the pain so it will go away. It's all mental."

"I'm going home, too," said Aileen. "I want to call my boyfriend to discuss our glorious win." She started up the stairs.

"Use our phone. Stay. I'm sure somebody will show up. Stay and meet the press."

"Besides, we didn't win. We tied," said Polly, putting on her coat.

"Same difference," said my mates.

"No, it's not the same. You could have won in the final quarter. You are the better team. That game should have been finished—played to the gun."

Just then a handsome young guy in a black bushy beard and pea jacket groped his way down the half-lighted steps. He looked around the laboratory. "I told your principal and that dumb coach what I thought of them, too. And I might just tell my readers. Hello, I'm Ron Mergler. Swell game, girls."

"Manfred is the dimwit. Coach O'Hara isn't. He's the only one in the whole school who kept us from dancing. He helped our team. I love him!" I was angry, but how tough could I get with someone who had covered our game for a newspaper. I offered the guy some honey on a cookie. He took it. Then everyone began talking at once. Ronald Mergler turned out to be a sports reporter from the Washington *Herald*. He asked us a zillion questions about dancing, football, Rinehart's laboratory, and our future plans.

"What future? You observed the end of our future," Rinehart answered in disgust.

"Someday our ship won't come in," said E.J., making ready to go.

"Someday my prince won't come if I don't get home and call him." Aileen left with the others.

Rinehart showed Mr. Mergler his chemicals, some test tubes full of gunk. I sat there by the miniature hothouse watching the plants grow. I thought about all the plays I should have called. I'd probably played badly. I relived with satisfaction a hearty bash I'd given Fritz—right between the shoulder blades. Hope he bruises easily. I saw again E.J.'s perfect kicks. Three points. One point. Wish I'd gone to her camp and played soccer. But I could pass the ball and run with it. I thought ahead to the fox-trot. Manfred will stuff us back in the kitchen so far we won't find the softball field in spring. Ahead—three solid months of buffeting between Mrs. Butor and the meat slicer. Oh, the pain.

"If only the gym were finished," I muttered.

"What gym?" Mr. Mergler looked up from the microscope through which he had been examining "anti-energy germs."

"The Lee gym," said Rinehart. "It's being repaired —rebuilt, really. The girls lost their basketball season, then were shoved into dance class, and that's when Coach O'Hara came through with the lacrosse field. He loves football. Wants to see it played well by no matter who. He set up today's game because he felt we should keep playing. Incidentally, he's not dumb. He's my hero."

"Well, for all I know he's the *dorf trudel*. I came to your party because he wouldn't talk to me. Just said 'No comment, no comment,' when he went into Manfred's office. I hung around, but when he appeared he brushed me off as if I were a little leaguer in the path of a Green Bay fullback. 'No comment'! Doesn't he know I'm a reporter?"

"He wouldn't care. He doesn't need reporters." Rinehart handed Mr. Mergler a book Coach had lent him.

"*Broken Field Running.* Fine piece of writing by a great runner, Knute Savage. Well, anyway, your principal gave me an eager interview."

"Naturally," I said. "Old Manfred craves publicity. He wants me to win the county spelling bee so he can stand beside me when I'm photographed in a chiffon evening dress," I said, rubbing my painful knees.

"Yes, he spoke of you. Suzanne, he calls you. He hopes you'll 'channel your energy and talent into more ladylike pursuits.' "

"Did he mention twirling and glockenspieling?"

"He did, and I quote again: 'Dancing will make a darling out of Suzanne. She'll be a marvelous majorette.' He wants me to write an article about Mrs. Butor's service to the community. He's very keen on her. What's she like?"

"Bring an extra large camera," Rinehart put in.

"Look," I said, "Cover the saddest story of the decade. Find out what cretin decided our gym needed repairing during basketball season. Find out which official couldn't wait until summer. Then urge your readers to send the guy off to a nut clinic."

"I have a better idea," said Mr. Mergler. He turned and headed up the stairs. I hobbled out later after another round of honey and Tang.

Monday morning Coach O'Hara came to chorus. Miss E. wasn't a bit happy to see him. She thinks sports waste time that should be devoted to singing. But I once tried to explain to her that basketball was singing with the body instead of with the voice, and she caught on. She may not like sports, but she's smart.

Coach asked for me. I went with him *allegro moderato con brio*.

"Zan, I want you to get the girls together and walk over to my house today at the time you usually practice. You know where I live—just off Blueridge Court. Bring Rinehart."

"What's up, Coach?" The last time I'd seen him he'd been fuming at Manfred. Today a calm man strolled with me down the hall.

"I plan to show films of your unfinished game with the Captains. I went over them myself yesterday. Good show. Catch-11 should see it. You'll learn a lot."

"A lot of what?" said doubting Teeny when I told her later. But she agreed to watch. E.J. guaranteed that all our faults would be on display.

"At camp I saw films of my tennis game. Painful way to learn. You end up making fun of yourself. But sure, I'll come."

"Oh, boy! I will analyze each play." Rinehart seemed elated.

We all sat together in the darkened living room watching tiny strangers fluttering on a yardstick. The second time through, my eyes adjusted to the small scale and I could follow the ball. Players began to squeal in recognition of themselves.

"EEEEEEk! Do I look awful in that tacky sweat-shirt!" Aileen covered her eyes. She looked again and laughed. "My bottom's up in the air. Isn't there some other way to center the ball?"

"Who's that five-by-five toad malingering on the ground? Ugh. It's Millie. Get up, Mil. Run with the ball."

"I see a hippopotamus playing right linebacker. Oh, it's just Joan. Let's put her in the yearbook!"

"Wish I were taller and faster," I said as I saw myself scrambling. Inches taller, and I could be a drop-back passer. Throwing out of the pocket is safer. With all that protection I wouldn't have these banged-up knees.

"Coach, that putrid lineman was off side for three plays in a row. Why didn't you call it?"

"And I saw both their halfbacks in motion before the snap. Isn't that illegal?"

"Check Fritz evading E.J. on their quarterback option. How did it happen?"

"Run the film back and I'll show you," said E.J. "That hunk of a pulling guard is holding me so I can't get through." She turned around and asked Coach to run the film again. We watched in silence until the final play—E.J.'s extra point that tied the game. With that I led a cheer. Coach rethreaded the projector in the dark. So far he had said nothing. He flicked it on once again and began a brisk monologue.

"Now that you've learned how to follow the ball, brace yourself for a critique. E.J., Polly. You other pass catchers. You've gotten into fancy-dan habits. You're leaping for the ball. Fine for modern dance and volleyball but wasted on the field. Run under the ball. Don't leap for it. While you're in the air you're losing time to gain on the ground. And since you're all right-handed, catch the ball over the right shoulder, using your left hand as the major catching hand. Watch yourselves again. Dropping passes! See what I mean?"

He rewound the film and reran some pass plays. He'll start on me next, I thought, massaging my puffy ankle. And he did.

"Zan, you're poised. You don't panic when those blockbusting linemen rush you. Fine. You're a good ball handler. Here comes an excellent fake and pass . . . right there!" He stopped the film with that compliment. I saw myself frozen in mid-air with my arm cocked over my ear. Then the ball sharpshot downfield. Next to me Rinehart took endless notes.

"Good girl," he breathed.

"Yes, your passing dazzles. Makes you a hero, a tiny bomber. But the ground game wins football games. It's meat and potatoes. You called too few running plays. That was your worst mistake."

Rinehart peered at Coach in the dark and said, "Well, we completed more passes than the Captains did. Fritz would sell his left arm to be able to throw like Zan. I bet even Randy can't . . ."

"Rinehart," interrupted Coach O'Hara, "statistics go in record books to look pretty. Winning's the important thing—the only thing. Your team *did not win*."

Rinehart scrunched down on the couch. He shut up.

"Laziness. That's what it comes down to. You find pass plays easier—all of you. With the pass only two or three key players have to be coordinated. But a running play requires split-second timing from six or seven of you. Watch these." He threaded the machine with a film of his own team. We watched the Generals run the sweep about twenty times. "You, left end. Don't let the opposition around. Stop their man at the line. Right tackle and fullback. You work together as one. You've got to keep their left end and middle linebacker from penetrating our backfield. For the sweep to work, their ends can't shoot the gap. First guard—pull hard to clear the fullback's move."

"My move," Millie put in.

"Second guard—look for the hole and seal it. Just stand there. Center—cut off their tackle. Run him backwards. Flanker, look for their left safety, wherever he is. Don't let him cross our line of scrimmage. Halfback—run hard until you get the ball from Zan. Then hold on to it and follow your blocking. If everyone does her job you're off for a big gainer. Watch how the boys do it."

We watched the sweep over and over. Okay, they run it perfectly. My cuts smarted. My arms seemed limp and heavy. My eyelids drooped. We, too, might master the ground game some year when Manfred falls off the Washington Monument. But the season ended with our tie. Today's a one-day reprieve, then goodbye pigskin, hello cha-cha-cha.

Now the room was pitch black. We hunched together waiting for the next reel; further abuse. Finally I said, "Coach, when I ran the option against the Captains I couldn't get past their linebackers. They knocked me down every time. I didn't have a chance."

"That's the way of this game," Coach replied. "They'll try to hold you. You've got to dodge them, get around them somehow. Get by them. Do a little juke step and buzz by them. Put a move on them." He feinted to his left, shifting around the projector.

"I can't do that, Coach."

"You do it or I'll bench you. You'll sit out the Dogwood Bowl!"

I heard Rinehart's clipboard hit the floor. Then silence. Then a click. Light flooded the room. Coach stood there smiling.

"Defense, this time we're gonna play bump and run with them. We can do it."

"The Dogwood Bowl?"

"Backfield, ends. The quickest way to get loose from a defensive back in order to catch a pass is to run straight at him. When you get on top of him, cut right or left. Naturally he'll follow you. He'll run alongside you at an angle. You'll gain a stride on the pass defender and that's all you need. Zan will zoom the ball right into your hands."

"In the Dogwood Bowl?"

"Runners—you've got to smell the goal line. Once it's in your nostrils you'll fight for every inch on your way to cross it. Second effort. Give me third effort."

"Girls can't play in the Dogwood Bowl," Rinehart finally blurted while ducking to retrieve his clipboard.

Coach glowered. "Girls *will* play in the Dogwood Bowl. Report to the parking lot on Saturday at 6:00 P.M. A school bus then takes you to Alexandria's Jefferson Stadium. The Generals versus the Richmond Redskins begins at 7:00 P.M. The game between Catch-11 and the Redskins' J.V. will take place at the half. Twenty solid minutes of football. This time we *will* win—in front of thousands."

The Dogwood Bowl. Jefferson Stadium. Redskins. Team bus. Bowlbuskinstadium. Richjefferredwood. Night game at half time. A spell had been cast over us all. Sorcerer O'Hara pushed the projector aside. He summoned us from voodooland.

"You girls with injuries from Friday—lumps, bumps, charley horses, whatever. I want to take a look at them. Come tomorrow to my office before you practice. I'll put you through the boys' training room while they're on the field. After that you can use Lee Stadium with the lights. You must get accustomed to the glare."

We floated out into a mild wind, and Rinehart finally found his voice.

"Whiff's cleared my head. For a while Coach had me mesmerized. Jefferson Stadium—hmmmm. More spectators hang out there than at any science fair." We broke into two's and three's, heading home. "Review your playbooks tonight, mates. Get your moms to buy honey. And let's think up better uniforms. Jeans are too tight to run in." Rinehart raised his fist. "Don't worry, we won't mess around with a tie again. We'll win."

"How do you suppose Coach did it, E.J.?" I asked as we angled through Ballston subdivision, heading for Military Road.

"Manfred dropped dead. How else? I'm running out for a pass. Toss me your history book." E.J. broke across a lawn.

"Did you see him in school today—Manfred, I mean?"

"See him? Has anyone, ever? Come on. Work *your* magic. Toss it." I gripped *The Awakening of Minorities: Militants on the Move* and threw for the boondocks.

Chapter 11

Dr. Ableson, the Generals' team physician, met us in the boys' training room. "Keep your slips on, girls. I'll take pulse, listen to hearts, and check whatever ailments hang over from last week's game. I must certify to your principal that you are all in the pink for football." He began with Aileen. "Pretty girl like you wants to play ball? Don't answer. Sit still while I thump." He listened.

I didn't. I was too busy looking around the castle. Seated on naugahyde rubdown tables, my fellow footballers reminded me of pampered movie stars. Underfoot, crimson wall-to-wall carpeting ran out of sight. Where? Into the shower room? Posh knows no limits! Piles of thick towels with "Lee Generals" embroidered in sky-blue lay on stools lining the far wall. Banners and pennants almost hid the recently painted pearl-gray wall: "Class 'A' District Title Holders"; "Old Dominion Football Hall of Fame"; "Governor's Apple Blossom Tournament"; "Randy Boyle, Greater Washington First String." And that padded door over there. Must lead to the ravaged gym. I tuned back in, listening for the sound of hammers.

"Don't you feel somewhat overweight, Miss Murphy?" The doctor prodded Millie's back with his stethoscope. She giggled.

"She's just right for a fullback or tight end," I said. "She's all toned up. No flab. Notice *that* while you're at it."

No, that door couldn't lead to the gym. I hear whirring saws in the other directions. Instead, maybe it goes into our own locker room dungeon. I thought about the girls' side, a hodgepodge of unlockable lockers, rotting benches, mildewy shower curtains, pitted asphalt floors throughout. Not even a throw rug. When did *we* ever get towels? Not even a washcloth. Or Kleenex. A cluttered dump with a rancid smell, that's what. Peeling paint, cracked tiles ...

"Miss Hagen, you're next ... Miss Hagen!"

I lifted myself out of the plush. I stood up.

"Oh, what a wee one! And they tell me you quarterback. Can you lift the ball?"

"I throw from a stretcher. Sometimes I wear stilts. I stand on a Coke box like Mickey Rooney. Take a look at my mashed ankle." I stuck it out in all its pulpy glory. Dr. Abelson, the oaf, bent over. I was tempted to give him a karate chop to the back of his head, but just then Coach came in.

"Don't worry about their bruises and bangs, Doctor. I'll put the whole gang in the whirlbath right after they've taken a sauna for their kinks. Take towels, girls, and come on."

Through the padded door Coach O'Hara led Catch-11. Wow! More wall-to-wall—everything.

"When I leave, get undressed," he ordered. "Wrap yourselves in towels. Go in the right door there to the steam room or over through that one to the sauna, which is dry heat. Sit down for as long as you can stand the temperature. Then take a cold shower, go back to the heat, and repeat until you hear my whistle. Then dress for practice and wait till I come in."

Oh, that steam. I settled into torpor. I felt my knots loosening, my aches lessening. All my welts receded as I watched droplets forming on the ceiling. I started counting them . . . hut one . . . hut two . . .

"Remember how the water never gets very hot in the girls' shower?" Bumpy said, glistening with sweat.

"And our dripping faucet used to drive me bats," Polly murmured, sounding far away. I couldn't see her through the steam.

"I, for one, wouldn't even mind that stinking chlorine footbath if we were back in our own locker room for basketball season," I said, going out for an icy shower. Then again to the heat. I knew Mom would be glad when I came home cured of my welts, gashes, stings, and smarts. She worried a lot about injuries.

The whistle—fog horn—brought us to reality. When we were safely in our clothes, Coach asked if anyone still could find a pain. I mentioned my ankle. E.J. held up a black-and-blue wrist. Teeny suddenly felt a cleat mark. Coach sent our teammates to practice with a warning to study their assignments for running plays.

"Hit your playbooks. You three stay. Into the whirlpool. Sit on these chairs. Zan, dangle your foot and leg into this end. You, too, Teeny. Eleanor, put your whole arm in the water." The motor thrummed as water spun around the tub. What a life! An athlete's cure-all. I counted bubbles . . . hut one . . . hut two.

After a while I said, "How'd you do it, Coach?"

He caught on right away. "Not me. Well, at least, not completely me. Your friend the reporter helped get the game. He won over Mr. Manfred by promising him worldwide coverage, wire-service photographs, an international front page. The works. That kind of rot. Publicity for Lee High."

"Now it seems we'll have to beat the 'Skins so old

Manfred can pose with me in my helmet. We must win this one for the Dripper."

"For my part, I promised Mr. Manfred an injury-free game," said Coach. "You'll be wearing shoulder pads, padded football pants—Lee's J.V. uniforms. And plenty of tape."

"Baldy's finally coming around," I said. "Maybe he'll find us a gym somewhere."

"I also promised him that you'd all go back to dancing right after the Dogwood Bowl," Coach went on. "You'll have to keep that pledge for me." We three water babies grouched about that. Coach ignored us. "And something else you should know. Although Mr. Manfred seems pleased about your football spectacle, the bandmaster's livid. His kids will march only before and after the Generals' game —quite a comedown from a televised half-time show. I hear his featured majorette, Ruby Jean Twilly, is gunning for you."

"She can darn well spin her silver shaft over on the sidelines for a change—this time for the girl's team. My foot's better, Coach."

"My wrist, too."

"Relax them both in the water for a few more minutes. You know, Richmond's J.V. beat Lee J.V. in September. Their guys may not be as tough now after a month's layoff, but don't expect easy sledding. You need to practice hard this week. And I want you to take my scouting report of them home for study tonight. Get Rinehart to print up the highlights for your playbooks. Read carefully to find their weaknesses. Then make a game plan to exploit those very faults." Coach took down a small blackboard from the wall and brought it over to the waterside. "This is what I mean: if you read that their defensive backfield red-dogs a lot, you'll want to throw quick passes over them." He drew the play.

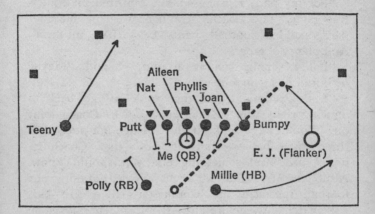

"You may discover from the report that certain of their linemen miss assignments. We'll run plays through those positions if that's the case. Okay, now out to practice. If you haven't recovered completely by tomorrow I'll put you under the baking lamp."

The water eddied, then smoothed out. I made a final survey of the room. No broken slats on their Venetian blinds, I noted. Maybe someday if our girls Dogwood-Bowled it up—annually—the school board would buy us a new foot bath, one without six inches of squishy moss all over it. I went out to practice.

ing our helmets and ending the song we'd sung all the way to Alexandria.

> Lee girls will shine tonight,
> Lee girls will shine.
> Lee girls will shine tonight,
> All down the line.
> We're gonna win tonight,
> We'll hold that line.
> When the sun goes down and
> the moon comes up.
> Lee girls will shine.

Naturally, we made "girls" out of "boys."

> Football ... Football ...
> Football ... Boys
> You play football,
> We'll make the noise.

Pregame hoopla. Cheerleaders tumbled all over each other, whipping up the capacity crowd. Kathy Sue Lathem, the Generals' mascot, cartwheeled, flipped, rolled, then snapped her fingers at the thousands who followed her idiotic moves. No one noticed us as we slunk into our prearranged seats on the fifty-yard line—Row "A"—next to the band section. The bandsmen were still on the field, right now forming their block-letter "LEE." They'd practiced three months for that? Kathy Sue strutted in front of the brass section, handspringing now and then from trumpet to trombone. Pick her up, someone. Beat the bass drum with her dumbbell head. Feh.

"Crackerjacks, popcorn, rootbeer, redhots . . ."

"Don't buy any of that junk, team," Rinehart advised. "It will churn in your stomach, ruin your tim-

ing." He placed himself in our midst and passed out
Chiclets. "Here, chew, get rid of your tensions."

So we chewed. We leaned back in our overcoats,
chewing and watching some kids selling banners.
Triangular blue and gray pennants saying "Lee Generals" blew in the stiff breeze above our side of the
field. I wished that Catch-11 had a huge dazzling flag
up there. I took off my scarf, stood up, and waved
furiously. Lurleen Dewey waved back from the field,
dipping and prancing toward the sidelines. She froze
in an arabesque, raised her baton to salute. Salute
what? Zowie, there's Miss E. What's she doing here?
She hates football. She climbed a portable platform,
lifted her arms . . . "Ladies and Gentlemen, sing your
National Anthem."

The Generals high-stepped onto the field, passing
through a double line formed by our drum and bugle
corps. Flourishes of drumsticks, handshaking among
Generals and Redskins, coin flipping . . .

"Ladies and Gentlemen, Eugene Matello will kick
off to the Generals."

I hoped to steal pointers for our own game, so for
one quarter I followed each play. Rinehart kept up a
rapid commentary. He sure understands football. To
hear him talk you'd believe he could actually throw
the ball. By the second period I began to lose interest
in the zero-zero slugging match. I scanned the crowd.
I waved to Fuzzy Harrison up by the press box. I
clapped to keep warm. I took dozens of deep breaths
to expand my lungs for the action. I waved to Mom
and Dad down on the Generals' thirty-yard line.
They had dragged along my brother Homer to
"watch your sister win." He seemed to be sulking. I
opened my special Dogwood Bowl program, perusing
the contents. I skipped over to the Generals' picture,
a huge center-fold-out. No staples pierced their uni-

forms. They looked sternly at the photographer and seemed to say, "We're invincible." Then an action shot of Randy standing in the air, grinning toothily while throwing one of his five-yard specials. Ech. Team statistics, a tribute to the yell squad, a full-page glossy photo to F. Parnell Manfred . . . say, where's the announcement of our game?

A roar from our crowd told me the Generals had finally scored. "Randy's done it again," said Rinehart. "Take your coats off, team. Let's go down to the sidelines. Half time's about to begin."

> He's our guy
> He's our dream
> Randy's captain
> Of our team.
>   Yea!

"Ladies and gentlemen. Tonight for our half-time extravaganza, a really really big show. Something really really . . . uh . . . different, folks. Yes, sir-*ree,* the First Annual Mini-Dogwood Bowl. With the lovely Lee Generalettes versus the Richmond Babyskins."

"Generalettes? Rinehart, for Pete's sake, send Bumpy or one of the subs up there to that dodo's microphone and give him our team's name." I pointed to the press box. A familiar beard smiled at me. By his side, sat F. Parnell Manfred, microphone in hand.

"There's nothing we can do about the name now," Rinehart said. "Come on, let's get ready to take the field."

Manfred spoke again. "Yessir-*ree,* these saucy little girls will give you twenty spunky minutes of football in a game against the Richmond J.V.s."

The upstaged marching band enjoyed their rest. They reclined against their instruments, pointing to us when Manfred finished his introduction. Ruby Jean Twilly appeared to be having a fit of apoplexy as we ran onto the field.

We gathered at our bench, which was still cluttered with General's gear. I pushed aside dirty towels, crunched paper cups, balled-up blankets and raincoats, broken shoelaces, rolls of tape, and a megaphone. Then I jumped up on it.

"Lookit, everyone, our night has come. In twenty minutes we can show all these people that Lee girls are to be reckoned with. We can beat these guys. I know we can."

Rinehart shouted, "Hear, hear," and got out his daily log to read us a pep talk he'd copied from Knute Savage. But just then Richmond stormed from the far bench. I watched a mass of hot-water-bottle red uniforms taking their places to kick off. Catch-11 lined up.

All at once the ball whizzed by my nose. "I got it," said Millie, chugging up the sideline to the thirty-five before a Redskin could cop her handkerchief.

"First and ten." We had a genuine referee and an actual chain crew stood by.

I called a quick opener. Six yards. A little swing pass to Polly worked for five and a first down. I saw the J.V. linemen eye each other. They seemed puzzled. Another pass to Polly, this time over the center, then Millie went off tackle for our second first down. Back in the huddle I wetted a finger to test the wind. It hadn't bothered short passes. Guess I'd try another, since the J.V. had seen my sucker trick of testing the wind. They'd now think I was going for the long one.

"E.J., they might blitz this down. Try to scare us.

I'll throw you a screen pass as they blow in."

"Their middle linebacker's a bully," she said. "He's already given me a clip or two. Throw to the right side."

I did, but just a little high. E.J. got her hands up, bobbled it a sec, then hung on. She ran fifteen yards, and we suddenly found ourselves on their twenty-five yard line.

"We can score from here. Let's run the sweep. Everyone, do your duty so Millie can leg it on in. Listen for the short count, then throw some hard-nosed blocks." Millie took my handoff as the two guards pulled from the line. She cleared right end, following Nat and Phyllis perfectly, then she cut to the inside. Their safety man tripped on his own elephantine feet, and Millie crossed into the end zone standing up. We lined up quickly for the extra point. E.J. did it again, a sidewinder kick right into the peanut gallery.

Seven to nothing, Catch-11. The J.V. called time out, took off their helmets and flopped down on the cold grass. I watched Rinehart prowl the sidelines. He signaled me over. "They don't know what's hit them yet, Zanner. Did you see Nat flatten that shrimpy linebacker? Now go in there and hold them. Try for a turnover. Make 'em fumble."

A ghostly silence had followed our points. I looked up now to the half-empty grandstands. They're out for Pepsies, I thought, and the sleeping ones await the pom pom girls. Hadn't anyone but Rinehart noticed our perfect sweep?

The Babyskins had. When we kicked off to them, they brawled up the field like a pack of desperadoes, leaving Nat and Phyllis in the dust. Their scatback reached our forty-five before we knew what hit us. They laughed and shouted to each other.

"I got one."

"I got another. I really chopped her. That makes two."

"Nine to go."

Nat crept off the field and JoJo came on. The crowd stirred a bit. They liked blood. On the first play from scrimmage I got the message, too. Some hippopotamuscle decked me hard, then stepped down on my left hand. Crunch! Lucky it was my left. He menaced me with a few choice words, too.

"Hey, Sweetie, want me to call you an ambulance? Okay, you're an ambulance." He laughed. I didn't. Their tight end yelled from the huddle, "You'll need an iron lung when I've run over you, you pushy dames."

They lined up in the shotgun. We'd never practiced against it, but I recognized the formation from our playbook. I called over my shoulder. "Watch a pass. Watch for a pass, everyone." Their receivers flooded our backfield, bumping us hard coming by. A catch to the fifteen. Then a delayed buck to the five. On that one a Lilliputian flanker tried for my other hand. I cuffed him and grabbed the handkerchief.

"Mighty fierce out there just now," said Phyllis, sitting down in our defensive huddle.

"They've figured out we aim to win. One guy whumped me on that last down." E.J. rubbed her neck.

"Some mean boy broke my ankle bracelet," Aileen mourned. "Ripped it off. It's gone."

I heard a few weak voices from the bleachers saying. "Hold that line, girls. . . . Push 'em back. Generalettes." I cringed and got ready for a goal-line stand. First and five. A straightahead. Aileen lunged for their halfback as he tried to come through the line. She got him, too. Next, another plunged right up the middle. This time I popped in the hole between Aileen and Phyllis and snatched the handkerchief from the guileless fullback. Third and three, until a quarterback sneak took the J.V. to our one-yard line. What will they do now? Try for six points or kick a field goal? "Go for it, go for the touchdown, you yellow 'Skins." The bleachers had sprung alive. The Richmond center came up over the ball, ready for a short snap to his quarterback. They would try for six. "Hold that line, girls. Hang in there." More voices from the end zone.

"Ready, set . . ."

Joan jumped off side and the referee ran in to call a penalty. He inched the football closer to the goal. Fourth and millimeters. "Hut, hut." Another sneak. What an imagination on that quarterback. We stopped him cold before he could lift a shoe.

We took over the ball on our one-yard line. What a hole to be in—nowhere to fade, nowhere to disappear. A false wiggle and they'd drop me in my own end zone for a safety.

"I'd better not pass from here. They'll cream me for two points. Let's try to run through them."

"Their left tackle keeps grabbing my face mask," Millie complained. "Maybe the ref will see him some year."

"I'll tell him during the next time out." I said. "Okay, everyone, we need some elbow room."

I called the quarterback draw. I stepped back as if to pass from the pocket. Millie, Polly, E.J., and our two ends moved out for the pass—decoys. While the J.V.s dropped off the line to cover the receivers, I bumped forward through the center. Aileen made a key block, I rambled for ten yards, and the first period expired with the gun. As we strolled to the far end of the field, I asked the referee to look for face-masking.

"I've missed that, girls. But I won't next time. You're playing well. Too bad no one's watching. They'll be sorry when they read about your skill in the newspaper. There's a reporter over there taking pictures." Sure enough. Mr. Mergler sat on our bench with Rinehart, Nat, Charlotte, and some other old men. Reporters? They all waved and made encouraging faces. Our only fans.

We huddled. I suggested the fullback dive from the "I" formation, Rinehart's last-minute addition to our playbook. The linemen had forgotten their assignments, so I drew the dive in the chalky end zone.

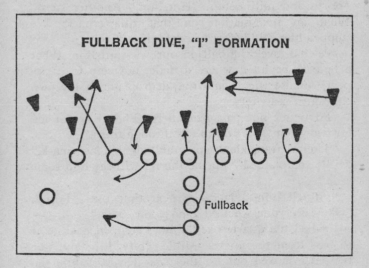

FULLBACK DIVE, "I" FORMATION

The second quarter started. We lined up in the "I." I took the snap, spun around, and handed off to Millie, who roiled through a fast-closing hole and into their defensive secondary. As she tried to twist by their free safety, he slapped the ball from her hand and fell on it seconds later—a recovered fumble on our own fifteen-yard line. We'd have to hold them again.

But we didn't. Their halfback alternated off tackle to the right, then left. For three. For five. A short square-out pattern by their fat tight end and the ball thrown right on the button brought them to our one again. We stood fast through yet another quarterback sneak, a crossbuck, then a broken play. On the fourth down, their quarterback buffeted Phyllis for six points. He added the extra point, tying the score. Well, anyway, by now the entire end zone bleacher crowd was awake and cheering for us to hang on, to stop them. When we didn't hold the line they yelled, "Go get it back, girls."

Aileen took their kickoff and charged to our twenty-yard line, where she met seven red jerseys. They skirmished for the handkerchief, sending her breathless, shaken, ragbaggy out of bounds. She landed spread-eagle in front of our bench. Pop! Pop! Pop! Flashbulbs exploded. Back in the huddle Aileen said, "Let 'em scalp me. I don't care. I'll get my picture in the paper. Onward." So I called running plays, a pitchout to E.J., a lateral to Millie, a Z-in pass to Tccny at right end.

Midfield. We'd made it there by methodical exactness, precision. Coach would be proud of our ball control. We inched forward some more. Short passes, shorter runs. Three yards and a cloud of dust. We took turns colliding with their huskies, who grew rougher on each advance. My left hand seemed stiff and blown up—my own case of elephantiasis. The minutes trickled away. I wanted to score before the half because I knew we'd gain a psychological advantage over the J.V.s by going to our bench ahead in points. I called time out.

"Polly, remember your catch in our other game? When you hauled in the long one? I'm going to try it again. Break downfield quickly and take a position in the right side of the end zone. You linemen, stand fast. Give me a few extra seconds. Zone block if you have to."

"They've been giving me double coverage on the last few plays, so Polly might get absolutely free," E.J. whispered.

A desperation pass, that's what! I shouldn't have thrown it, off balance as I was. With one defender gripping my shoulder, another about to seize the handkerchief, I let fly a teetering pass right into their cornerback's breadbasket. He exploded back at us, going almost all the way with his interception. The half ended with our usual tie.

Chapter 13

We weren't grumpy on the bench, just busy. Buddy had come out from the boys' half-time preparations to help us with equipment.

"You'll play better if I cut off all these bunchy sleeves."

"My wrist needs tape."

"Me too."

"My lip's bleeding."

"Mine too."

"Oh drat, these shoelaces busted."

"Look at my hand, Rinehart." I said. "You think it's broken?"

"Can you move the fingers?" asked Mr. Mergler, squeezing my thumb with one hand and taking a close-up shot with the other. The flashbulb left me blinded for a second. My left hand felt like a mingle-mangle of hamburger and mashed potatoes.

Buddy snipped away at our jerseys. We hitched up our pants, tightened belts, and sucked on the oranges Rinehart had provided. The grandstands seemed full once again. I saw the bandmaster glowering at me through layers of smoke and blare. His sax man blew a catcall at us.

"Zan, I read about their quarterback in the program." Joe Donn Joiner's his name. He's being groomed for their first string next year." Mr. Mergler scurried around giving me advice while taking pictures.

"He'll never make it unless he learns to mix up his plays." I said. "No imagination. We've seen a billion quarterback sneaks already in ten minutes." I jumped up and down to keep from getting stiff while we waited. I tested the wind again. Gone down to nothing. Couldn't blame my intercepted pass on a zephyr. My own greedy fault.

"Keep an eye on him anyway." Rinehart advised. "Their coach could always send in a brilliant play."

The band cheered our return to the field. Confetti swirled in the end zones as the bleacherites came alive again. E.J. got off a long boot to a Tiny Tim, who ran it back for good yardage. Before we knew what hit us, their moose fullback, on the second play from scrimmage, lashed through our line, then through the secondary, and without breaking stride flowed onto pay dirt. A mild "Yipee" came from the crowd, but it was overpowered by an explosive "Block that kick, block that kick, block that kick. You can do it." We dynamited out of the huddle, encouraged by the cheering. Their right guard looked up at me from his three-point stance.

"We're gonna hash you on this one, GIRL."

"Try it, beanhead," I raged, jumping high just after the snap. I felt the ball ricochet off my one good hand. It bounced dead, short of its target, but the J.V. now led us, 13—7. Both my hands felt kaput, one swollen as big as a shot put, the other stinging and tingling unmercifully. Could I still chuck the ball? We'd see. My teammates came over to hug me for the save on the extra point. When we lined up for the kick-off, I heard Rinehart cheering from the sidelines.

Give me a Z.
Give me an A.

Give me a ZAN.
Give me a B.
Give me an A.
Give me a BALL.

ZANBALLER.
ZANBALLER.
Yea! Yea! Yea!

He flung his earmuffs in the air and jumped over the bench, tripping and landing in the heap of our overcoats.

For the next seven minutes we locked horns between our thirty and theirs. We'd run six plays and punt. They'd run six plays—three sneaks, two bucks, a screen pass—and punt. E.J. lofted three beauties—better kicks than the Redskins could muster. Each brought an ovation from our side of the field, where by now the cheerleaders cartwheeled into action for us. They tumbled. We tumbled, too. They leapt over each other, we leapt over the 'Skins. They clapped and shouted. We clapped to keep warm and shouted to each other "Atawaytogo, mate!" They released balloons to the sky. I released the football in another must-do pass. Batted down. I finally bored a spiral through the cold night air. Teeny caught it at their thirty. I looked at the clock: two minutes, thirty seconds to go.

Seven points, seven points,
Seven points more.
Come on, Generalettes,
Score, score, score.

The cheerleaders were handspringing and flight-leaping their darndest for us now. We couldn't lose.

I must not be intercepted. We mustn't fumble. Polly scooted for five on a trap play. We tried the sweep again, but Millie seemed to give up as she turned the corner. "Come on, Mil, don't hit and splatter. Keep your legs moving. Dodge 'em, dodgem," I shouted on the way back to the huddle.

"I'm too tired to center," Aileen panted, leaning against the circle.

"A few more hikes—only a few more, then . . ." The whistle blew. Five-yard penalty. Too much time in the huddle. Back to their thirty again. What will we do? What should I call?

By now the Varsity Generals had returned to the field. Lined up ready to reoccupy their battleground, pep talks ringing in their ears, they paid no attention to our drama. They seemed to be sneering. As I took my position behind Aileen, I saw Rinehart flailing his arms at them, urging them off our sidelines. He must be expecting an end run or an out-of-bounds pass. Yes, that's right. We had to get out of bounds each play from here on in. That would stop the clock. With the snap I bluffed a handoff, then a pass, and headed to our side of the field. Expecting another desperation throw, the J.V. linebackers had dropped off to cover, to intercept. I breezed along just inside the chalk until a billy-goat gruff butted me out on the thirteen. I landed at Lurleen Dewey's feet. She greeted me with a pinwheeled figure eight, her torch baton burning perilously near my head. She pulled me up.

"Don't let those bullies win," she yelled "Score! Score!" She threw down her firebrand and led a cheer.

ZZZZZZZZZZZZZZZZZZZZ Z

ZZZZZZZZZZZZZZZZZZZZ   A
ZZZZZZZZZZZZZZZZZZZZ   N

Yea!

I dusted myself off, straightened my helmet, and stepped back onto the field. I called back to Lurleen.

"Our team is Catch-11, not Generalettes. Pass it on."

Thirteen stupid yards. Thirty-nine feet of chilly earth to cross for six points. In the seconds it took to count cadence the possibilities ran through my head. We're now losing. We might tie. No, not again! We could win with only seven little points.

"Hut. Hut. Hut. Hut," I rattled out to the right, but their gangbusters collected in front of me. I ducked left, then backwards. There. Ahead. There's some daylight. I started for it. I hurtled left, wrangled some running room, then was chased out of bounds on their two. This time I found myself tangled with a Richmond cheerleader who whispered, "Two more yards. You can do it. Beat 'em. Beat 'em." She's stabbing her own team in the back, I thought.

First and two. First and six stupid feet. Waves of entreaties from Lee's side of the field, sneaky encouragement from Richmond's. Polly stumbled for a foot, then I lost my footing and had to eat the ball. The official clock by the flagpole gave us nineteen seconds. I threw a jolter to Teeny, who dropped it, then dawdled back to the huddle more dejected than ever. The incompleted pass had stopped the clock. I've got to think, I told myself.

> Hey, hey,
> Ho, ho.
> Come on, Catch-11,
> Let's go.

I looked back at Rinehart and Mergler. The beard tapped his temple in exasperation. Think, he seemed to say. Use your noggin. Use it the way Joe Donn doesn't use his. Yea, that's it. No time for fanciness. Nothing razzle-dazzle. Nothing imaginative. I'll pull a sneak, Joe Donn's favorite weapon. We haven't tried one for 19 minutes, 42 seconds—the entire game. I winked at Mergler as Rinehart yelped like a one-man pep club.

ZIPPER
ZAPPER
ZOOMER
ZEPHYR
ZAMMER
ZINGER
ZANNER
ZAN

I called the quarterback sneak. I'd cannonball straight at them. I'd need good traction for a quick start. I glanced down at the nearly frozen dirt. Fine. Should I dive over or follow a blocking wedge of the center and guard through the line? I remembered the scouting report. I recalled that Coach had noted the J.V.'s right tackle held his shoulders so stiff, his head so high he probably wouldn't be able to dig in efficiently for a goal-line stand. In my brain the wedge began to percolate. If I stood up straighter than usual to take the ball from Aileen, I'd have a clear view, together with a split-second start on their linemen.

The crowd came apart as we broke huddle. "Onward!" they all screamed. "Onward, Catch-11!" I called the "hut s." My center and left pulling guard came off the football faster than I've ever seen two

linemen move. They wedged hard into their oppo-
sites. They moved their men outside, more by surprise than force. I punched through the opening,
slithered a foot—two feet—three feet—four—more, and
fell, landing in the end zone. The Redskins reeled
back, clutching their helmets, leaning on the goalposts, berating each other for letting me through. Our
fans drowned them out with an ecstatic wail: "Make
that kick. One more point. Make that kick."

When we came up on the line for the extra-point
attempt, the J.V.s were calm. Their friends, the Richmond Varsity team, supported them from the sidelines,
where they waited for the gun to end our mini-bowl.
Their own game would begin again in five seconds.
The linebackers hissed.

"You'll never make it. We've got it blocked already
and we're gonna kill ya."

And they almost did kill us while blocking E.J.'s
kick. Seven flyweights, lightweights, and middle-
weights vaulted over, slam-banged through the line,
cudgeling us aside with their heads and shoulders,
treading our linemen underfoot while groping for the
ball. Two heavyweights and two extra heavyweights
jumped on the others' backs, standing eight feet tall
to block the kick.

I heard the gun from under a pile of Redskins. It
sounded far away—like a cap pistol. The Dogwood
Bowl is over for us, I thought. We've tied again—for
our second and final game.

The varsity Generals and Redskins swept onto the
field, brushing our wounded aside. It was their field
now.

"Losers," called Randy, placing his kicking tee in
position.

"We're not losers, we're tie-ers," I shouted back.

"Guess we showed you. Go back to your knitting, freak!" said Joe Donn, slowpoking beside me.

"I've heard that before," I said. "Last time, in fact. Explain what you showed us." He started to tell me.

"I can throw furth—"

In that instant we both heard tumult from grandstands and bleachers. Everyone, everywhere.

"Keep playing!"

"Break that tie!"

"We want a winner!"

"Go another quarter!"

"BREAK THAT TIE!"

"Play sudden death!"

"Sudden-death overtime!"

"SUDDEN DEATH. SUDDEN DEATH."

Uproar. No, pandemonium. I straggled for our bench. I saw the game officials in conference at midfield. There's Mergler with them . . . and F. Parnell Manfred . . . and Coach O'Hara . . . good grief, there's Rinehart. Who are those others I've never seen before? I inched through the milling cheerleaders, majorettes, twirlers, pep clubbers, marching bandsmen, drum and bugle corpsmen, parents, well wishers —our fans. I had to sit down. I wanted to die.

Far away, up in the pressbox, I heard a voice: "Ladies and gentlemen. Catch-11 now meets the Redskins' J.V. in a sudden-death overtime."

Overtime? Overkill, he means.

Chapter 14

Sudden death. Instant life. A game extended, allowing us—or them—to break the tie. First team to score wins.

In the twinkling of an eye our gridiron cleared again. At the midfield stripe, game officials flipped another coin and Joe Donn drawled, "Tails." Tails. Hard luck. They'd receive.

"You win again, Donnsy boy," I laughed. "Guess you showed me."

"Eat your heart out, you bride of Frankenstein," he yelled. "This time we'll show you no mercy." He swaggered off the field.

I clenched my ailing fists. Some mercy! I returned to the bench for a two-minute break. Coach O'Hara joined us as our fans made the stadium vibrate. He looked around approvingly.

"Team, this is where conditioning pays off. Draw some deep breaths. Get your second wind. All those grass drills and sprints will pull you through now. Zan, how's the ankle? Holding up all right? Anyone else with an old injury? New one?" No one whimpered. We sat there sucking lemons and oranges while Coach delivered the shortest pep talk on record. "If you want this game, go get it. Go get the ball and score." He trotted off toward his own team, which waited angrily, impatiently, in the wings. Now it was long-winded Rinehart's turn.

"Listen. I'm gonna give you a play that we never practiced, a way we can get the ball before the J.V. runs even once from the line of scrimmage. The onside kick. A real game breaker. E.J., it's up to you at first. You've got to kick a short roller. Don't boom it, just push. It must go ten yards, at least, to be legal. Kick it so the up-front members of their team can't pick it up cleanly. Make it scriggly, goofy, the way the football was to us when we first started playing. The rest is up to all of you. As E.J.'s foot hits the ball, steam down the field at full throttle and someone—everyone—throw yourself on that ball. You hear me? Fall on that football. Charlotte, get warmed up. You're going in for Nat. We need a fresh blocker out there in case we get the ball."

"We'll get it," said Polly, "and then the game."

The field judge hailed us and blew his whistle. We didn't fiddle around. Catch-11 lit out and stretched across the field between our thirty-five- and forty-yard lines. E.J. set the ball on its tee, then stepped back. We waited. She ran forward. SSSSSSS—zilch. A perfect fizzle. A dud. We ran downfield as the ball made its ponderous, corkscrewy way to their forty-five, where fresh old Charlotte fell on it.

What now? Cower and hide, judging from the dragons' faces just a noseguard away. They're waiting for the sweep, the sneak, the run—waiting for me. We'll never make it on the ground. No way we're gonna get there.

Or will we? Yes, if we trick them again. "We're going with the fleaflicker." I announced on an impulse. "The double—no, triple reverse. Hut. Hut." I almost snatched the ball from Aileen, prodded right, and handed off to Polly. She moved to the left. Suddenly Teeny, at split end, turned around and ran toward Polly. Polly handed her the ball, Teeny running right. She faked out the Redskins. She faked out our Catchers. She even confused me. Finally snuffed out by a J.V., Teeny came to rest on their thirty-three. But when the smoke cleared, a penalty marker lay on the field. We'd been caught holding—fifteen yards. Fifteen big ones. Back to our own forty-yard line. We'd wasted our phantom raider.

Well, enough of this, I thought. My brain is ready to crumble from thinking so hard all this time . . . run here, go there . . . if their guard does this, do that . . . on hut two I pull left . . . should we shift into a single wing now or later . . . what's Joe Donn saying in his huddle . . . feint left, strike right. . . .

We mustered for the final time! I decided to hit those J.V.'s with TNT, an aerial to end all aerials. The halfback option. "On five, mates. Remember your assignments." I dropped the hiked ball, but it took a lucky bounce back into my arms. I lateraled to E.J. and then whizzed through the line. I stopped, turned around, and skidded backwards, watching E.J. sidestep, shimmy, flimflam around our backfield. "I'm here. I'm here. Chuck it to me," I called.

I jumped to catch her blooped toss to their forty-two. I hauled it down, clasped it hard, cut for the sideline as Joiner came up behind me. Almost neck and neck now. He reached for my handkerchief and I made a stutter step and . . . and . . . and . . . and . . . I danced across the goal line. I tossed the football high to the bleacher bums, then gathered with Catch-11 to hoist Rinehart to our shoulders. He pummeled our heads as we carried him to the bus. Mergler tagged along, toting his camera and typewriter.

Chapter 15

ZANNENBALL EXPRESS RAMS RICHMOND IN SUDDEN DEATH CONTEST

A Tale of True Grid as Coed Leads Lee Team to 19-13 Victory over Boys

BY RONALD MERGLER, JR.

Special to the *Herald*
ARLINGTON, Virginia, Dec. 7—The next face for the bubble-gum card collectors of great gridders should be Suzanne "Zan" Hagen, a grinning, gritty, tow-headed blonde quarterback-middle linebacker who led her team of former dance students to an incredible sudden-death triumph tonight. Playing in borrowed uniforms that dwarfed them, eleven girls from Robert E. Lee Junior-Senior High waxed the Richmond J.V. team in three minutes of overtime pyrotechnics that followed a hard-fought 13–13 tie after *four five-minute quarters.*

For twenty minutes Miss Hagen ran, passed, linebucked and linebacked with the poise, ability and spirit of a hall-of-famer. Then, in the most brilliant and unexpected maneuver of the game, she called the halfback option for Lee's second play from sudden-death scrimmage. Taking the handoff, Eleanor ("E.J.") Johnson (who had already kicked a soccer-style extra point, out-punted her male counterpart, and caught several key Zanballs) lifted a high pass to her own quarterback. Hagen seized the ball in a crowd of Richmond red shirts and whipsnaked along the sidelines, a half step in front of her rival quarter-back, Joe Donn Joiner, who had already spent a futile evening in the wake of this whirlwind. She crossed the goal line leagues ahead of him. Shazan!

An earlier bolt from the blue-eyed wrecker had come in the fourth period when Miss Hagen scored on the quarterback sneak, a play repeatedly used by the baby Redskins to little avail. She also blocked an extra-point attempt in a valiant jump and typical Zannerism that left her right hand useless. But not for long.

A well-balanced team organized and coached to perfection by Lee science-whiz Arthur Rinehart, Catch-11 (as they prefer to be known) proved that athletic ability, game-brains, imagination, superb conditioning, will, and second, third, and tenth effort, are not restricted to male athletes. Fearless end Teeny Miller stirred the capacity crowd with several timely catches in the tradition of Lance Alworth. Lineman Anne ("Bumpy") Bumstead provided the game-tying block for Hagen's sneak.

Michael O'Hara, coach of the varsity Generals, reported in an interview following his own 10–10 Dogwood Bowl tie with Richmond that he had held occasional skull sessions with the girls but that "Arthur Rinehart basically is responsible for getting his team physically and mentally ready for tonight's win." O'Hara takes credit only for the girls' initial interest in football, which they decided to play, at his suggestion, in their P.E. class rather than attend required dance sessions. O'Hara further stated that he only wished Zan Hagen had quarterbacked his own team, "for then my boys would not have been humiliated. She's a Zan-of-all-trades—a winner." He added that he would take "any of the rest of those girls, too," and claimed a football dynasty at Lee since most of the girls are only freshmen and sophomores. Several key players, including Hagen, are eighth-graders.

After the game, I interviewed members of Catch-11 on the bus en route to their makeshift dressing room at Lee High School. Owing to the rebuilding of Lee's gymnasium, including the girls' locker facilities, the team used a basement boiler room for returning their uniforms and for a well-earned rest. Millie Murphy, who scored the game's first touchdown running the Lombardi sweep, and who played an outstanding game on defense, filled me in n the history of her involvement in football: "We rebelled against monkey suits and those idiotic ballet steps. When our basketball season collapsed along with the gym, we were sent off to dance class. Zan led us out of the kitchen and onto the playing field."

Petite center Aileen Dickerson took time out from posing for *Herald* cameramen to tell "the true miracle of finding my pearl I.D. anklet during a sudden-death huddle. I just looked down where Zan was drawing the reverse play and there it was in fhe dirt. That mean Laddie Griffen had torn it off me. Let's give a cheer for Zanballer."

And cheer they did. (For center spread photographs see p. B 12.)

(ED. NOTE: A three-part feature article on Hurricane Zannie and her Catch-11's, complete with a pro-type scouting report for each position, begins tomorrow. Also see Wednesday's Women's Page for a warm, human-interest feature: "At Home with the Hagens." Mrs. J. K. Hagen describes the meals in the exacting training menus she prepared for her daughter.)

* * *

Chapter 16

When the annual football awards banquet came around just before Christmas vacation, Catch-11 was there. I wanted us all to wear our uniforms, minus pads and helmets, of course, but we settled for dresses. I wore my brown wool jumper—my other dress. My Monday-Wednesday-Friday outfit. "Old Brown-Jumper Hagen," Rinehart calls me. Teeny wore taffeta, and Aileen bought her first formal, a mass of lace, tulle, and something that looked like spaghetti, all in Robert E. Lee colors.

We sat at huge oval tables squashed onto a tiny dance floor at Dino's restaurant. Big shots in the Arlington County Dads' Booster Club took long tables up above us on a platform. They chomped away on fried chicken and mashed potatoes. I could hear them telling jokes. I attacked my salad with one hand and waved the other at Ron Mergler up there next to Coach O'Hara and F. Parnell Manfred. They all waved back and smiled.

The boys didn't. They were furious. We icky girls had been invited to their very own stag party. Rumors that all of them planned to walk out if we appeared had flown around school. But here they were. Eating, too. I looked from table to table, watching a few Captains trying to shove peas through clenched teeth. Randy guzzled his water and stared crossly at our gang. I hadn't seen him up close since his Dogwood Bowl tie with Richmond. He seemed to be growing more pimples these days. Plus he had a big black and blue mouse under his left eye. Must be from basketball practice. Someone gouged him in the cheek with an elbow, I thought. But I envied him his mouse. I'd even take his rotten acne if only the girls could have a basketball season. Randy's whole offensive line was around him. They glowered at us right through the first two courses. Every now and then I'd catch a few wisps of their sarcasm. I didn't care. I cleaned up my plate. I waited for the apple pie. Next year if anyone asks me about food for the Boosters' banquet I'll recommend roast beef and chocolate soufflé. I sat back and listened to the first speaker, someone's dad from the Lions' Club. He croaked.

"... and in every ... uh ... football season ... uh ... there are ... uh ... surprises. This year we ... uh ... witnessed the ... uh ... unheralded rise ... of our ... uh ... varsity front four, sophomore boys ... uh ... who came off the ... uh ... bench, so to speak, and ... uh ... bloomed. Yes, that's it ... uh ... bloomed. Another unexpected ... uh ... pheee-nomenon ... proved to be ... uh ... Tommy Hickman, who ... uh ... developed into a bruising running ... uh ... back ... despite a crippling ... uh ... attack of gout in the stretch ... uh ... drive."

Gout? I heard that his teammates got jealous of all the newspaper attention he received and stopped blocking for him. Real prima donnas.

"... Uh ... Last but not ... uh ... least our ... uh ... girls' team. Who would have thought ... uh ... way back in September that ... uh ..."

That's just it. Who would have thought a bunch of girls could learn to manage a football? He rambled on, then finally quit for dessert. Coach O'Hara stood

now, ready to hand out the awards. Randy stopp[
joking about us to listen for his own name. No doub[
it would be called for the Most Valuable Player gold
medal. Waiters poured coffee for the players' parents.
Mothers had been invited this year. First time. High
time! I glanced at my mom and dad on the platform,
where for some bizarre reason they had chosen to eat.
There with the mucky-mucks. Next to the mayor.
Now that's class, I thought. I've got class parents.
They belong up there for all the help they've given
me during football season. Dad even admitted I
could call a game better than Homer. I guess he forgot my brother plays defense.

Dads and a few sons lit cigars as Coach warmed up
with the highlights from the General's season. He finally got down to business.

"For Defense Man of the Year, judged by his peers,
Ben Brown." Herculean clapping from the next
table.

"I could run by him," Millie remarked quietly.

"The Boosters' Silver Cup for the most improved
player . . . The Elks Club Linebacker Trophy . . .
And now, the scholar-athlete citation voted by Lee
teachers to that boy who, while playing varsity football, maintains the highest grade-point average."

While Dum Dum Cadden walked up to accept his
one hundred dollar savings bond, Rinehart swatted
me (under the table, of course) and said boisterously,
"Those same teachers gave me a measly five bucks
for winning the science fair this year."

"Sssssssssss. Shut up." From the Captains' table.

". . . and here with us to present the Mayor's
Medallion for Sportsmanlike Conduct, the Right
Honorable . . ."

The next voice I heard was Randy Boyle's, acceptıg, as he put it, "humbly this honor that means more to me than if I had won only on athletic ability." Feh. He returned to torment us, licking his lips, patting a damp stray lock of hair in place. He brushed his medallion past my temple. Apparently the mayor missed that tackle Randy laid on me at practice last month. Some sportsman. He'll be making his other trek up there to the head table to grab his M.V.P. Get set.

". . . So to the main events, I turn this portion of the program over to the *Herald* Associate Editor of Sports, Ronald Mergler, Jr. Ladies and Gentlemen, Ron Mergler."

When he came to the microphone, I noticed Mr. Mergler's spunky blue blazer with the Lee crest over the breast pocket. A genuine fan. He slipped a small package from a hip pocket and began speaking about the Most Valuable Player medal. Every eyeball rolled over to Randy. He beamed.

" . . . so after grave consideration of all factors involved . . ."

Randy started rising from his chair.

". . . the *Herald* sports writers and editors voted this . . ."

Completely upright now, Randy broke toward his medal.

". . . medal to Zan Hagen, whose skill, zeal, and imaginative signal-calling brought her team honor and victory in the Dogwood Bowl."

Oh, brother, I thought. Why did I wear this dumb brown jumper? I now have to show it to everyone in Dino's. I waded through a thousand backslappers. I tripped, then mounted the stairs. I somehow grasped the M.V.P. medal.

"Stay here. Sit down over by your mom," Mergler

hollered over the clapping. "Never mind a spee— You can save it for the *Herald* Tournament."

What could he mean? I teetered to my mother's side, "Hi, Mom."

"Finally, the Dogwood Bowl championship rings, donated by the Washington Area Press Club." He took a large box off the lectern and held up some rings. I peered out through the klieg lights at the Generals on the edge of their seats, cigar-smoke clouds shrouding their expectant faces.

". . . to the winners, not tie-ers, of that confrontation . . ."

But we won. We were the only winners!

"Catch-11."

Before I recovered my senses I had wrung the hand of everyone in sight. My ring—my first one ever—kept slipping off my thumb into the palms of mayors, Boosters, coaches, mothers, Lions, teammates, Elks, teachers, and even Randy, who tried it on, hissing. "Richmond could have took you if you'd of been playing real football—tackle football. They'd of beat your—"

"Don't be too sure," I said, grabbing back my treasure.

Now every Catch-11 stood on the platform, squinting in the spotlights while trying on rings in a vain attempt at fit. Only Rinehart's didn't fall off. "I'll wear it on my ankle," sighed Aileen, hitching up her formal for a measurement. "Now I can give my boyfriend back his football ring. I earned my own."

". . . And now I bring you . . . And now I present . . . Please, folks, return to your places for the finale of our program. . . . At this time I give you over to the worthy hands of everyone's favorite principal, a man who in his first year at the helm of Robert E. Lee has

.oduced two teams of Dogwood Bowl caliber . . ."

The crowd settled down.

". . . a man who—in the great tradition of Branch Rickey, who broke the color barrier in major-league baseball—broke the traditional barrier of girls' participation in football . . ."

Ice tinkled in glasses.

". . . a man of vision, a man of courage, a fighter for the just, a savior of the underdog . . ."

Cigar butts glowed.

". . . the man of the hour, F. Parnell Manfred."

Waiters pushed away carts of dirty dishes, beginning to clear the dance floor. What for? Five men in gypsy costumes and carrying instrument cases appeared on a small bandstand in the corner. A fiddling basketball team? Oh oh, they're tuning up. The Violinstars? Our principal took the mike.

". . . Thus you see, my dear parents and school supporters, we have winners here, and as my contribution to tonight's festivities I'd like to make the following two announcements. This afternoon I worked out a final contract with Wiggins Brothers Construction Company for completion of our gymnasium. George Wiggins himself promised his men's efforts day and night—around the clock—until the last floorboard is in place. The contract gives him until January second, the moment we return from our Christmas recess. With lots of effort on everyone's part, our girls will have a basketball season after all."

Oh Wow! I'm dying of happiness. I . . . My eyes sting. What's this clear fluid dropping out of them?

"For my second announcement I'd like to break yet another barrier. Tonight, for the first time in Booster history, a dance follows this awards session. Ladies and Gentlemen, the music will begin."

The lights dimmed. No, that's just Mrs. Butor passing in front of the spot on the way to the floor. Mr. Manfred came toward me.

"Most valuable player, Suzanne, will you do me the honor of giving me the first—"

"I won't dance. I won't dance!"

Rinehart beckoned from the door. I bolted, zigzagged through the waltzers, and joined my coach for some basketball planning. I called over my shoulder:

"Zanballer won't dance!"

Rinehart's Playbook

A Football Glossary
for Beginning Players

Backfield: All players who aren't linemen—like half-backs, fullbacks, quarterbacks.

Blitz or Red Dog: It's a surprise, really. When one or more defenders in the defensive backfield (like line-backers or corner backs) charge across the line of scrimmage to tackle the passer. Usually they leave the pass rush to the defensive line. But not in the blitz.

Block: Butting into an opponent in order to keep her from getting to your ball carrier. To block, keep arms close to your body. You can also block by just standing still and looking mean or moving around only slightly. This keeps the defender from running through you.

Blown Play or Broken Play: When your own teammate (or several of them) forgets what she is supposed to be doing right in the middle of a play. Like if E.J. ran out for a pass at the very second she is supposed to be kicking a field goal.

Bomb: A very long and high pass thrown to gain a lot of yards.

Bootleg Play: The quarterback takes the snap, then fakes a handoff to the fullback or halfback, hides the ball on her hip and sweeps around end.

Bread-and-Butter Play: A team's best play, their favorite one. It's the play that gets yards every time, like the Generals' sweep.

Buck: To carry the ball right smack into the defensive

line, trying to bust through the defenders by using sheer strength rather than deception.

Bump and Run: It's when a defensive back lines up head-on the receiver and bumps into her to disrupt her pass pattern, then runs step-for-step with her to cover any other pattern she might run.

Center: The girl on the line who passes the ball through her legs to a backfield girl, usually the quarterback. The center starts each play. She is often an unsung hero in a game just by being a hard-working, steady player. When she hikes she looks like she's standing on her head.

To Center, Snap, or Hike the Ball: When the center begins the play by passing the ball from the ground through her legs to a backfield girl.

Call: To decide what play to make. The quarterback calls the plays in the huddle.

Chain Crew: Some official men on the sidelines who carry a chain hitched to some poles. They use it to measure how far the offensive team goes.

Chalk Marks: Every five yards on the field is a line of chalk. Also the field's boundaries are all lined in chalk. When a player goes out of bounds we can say, "She stepped over the chalk mark."

Clipping: To hit a defensive player from behind. Don't do it, because in a game you'll get your team a 15-yard penalty.

Conversion or P.A.T.: A one-point score made right after a touchdown by kicking the football over the crossbar between the goalposts. The conversion is sometimes called the "extra point."

Cut: To change your direction sharply when running.

Delayed Slant: A really tricky pass pattern. The receiver goes slowly a few yards across the line of scrimmage, then suddenly cuts at a 30-degree angle as fast as she can, running out for a pass.

To Double Team (or Double Coverage): When t
defenders guard one pass receiver. Not fair in girl
basketball, but in football it's fine, and sometimes
necessary if the receiver is especially speedy and smart.

Down: You get four downs to gain 10 yards. A down
starts when the football is snapped by the center and
ends when the official blows his whistle. He blows
it because the runner, receiver, passer, or kicker is
tackled, or is thrown out of bounds.

Downfield: The turf beyond the line of scrimmage. Used
like this: "She ran downfield as fast as her legs could
carry her."

Draw Play: Another tricky play. In this one the quarterback drops back, pretending to pass. As the defenders
rush in to dump the quarterback, she hands the ball
to one of the backs, who runs straight past the rushers.

Eat the Ball: This happens to a quarterback when she
is tackled while still holding the ball. She's looking
around for someone to pass to but all the receivers
are covered. Boom! She's thrown down while still
holding the ball.

End Zone: At each end of the field there's a zone where
the goalposts are. You have to get across the opponents' goal line, into their end zone, to score a touchdown.

Fade: When the quarterback steps quickly backward
after receiving the snap from center, that's fading.

Fake: To bamboozle the other team. For example, to
pretend to run when you're really going to pass. Or
to make a move to one side, but then actually running
in another direction.

Field Goal: A way to score three points by kicking the
football through the goalposts and over the crossbar.
For kicking, the ball is held in place upright on the
ground by a teammate of the kicker.

Fleaflicker Play: Any sort of wild, made-up play where

everal backs handle the ball before one finally runs or passes with it. The fleaflicker means to confuse the other team, but sometimes it confuses your own teammates as well.

Fly Pattern: To run straight down the field as fast as you can to catch a pass. That's flying.

Formation: The arrangement of players to begin each play. Like the T formation, the Split T, the I formation, and others you will learn.

Forward Pass: Any football thrown toward the defenders' goal line to a receiver.

Free Safety: A defensive back who roams around trying to intercept passes. You get winded often if you play this position.

Fumble: Where the football accidentally jounces out of your hands. Anyone can pick it up and run with it then. Try not to fumble. Hold on to the ball hard. Keep it snug against your body.

Game Plan: During the week before playing your Saturday game, your coach works out a plan of attack on your opponent. He figures out weaknesses in your opponent's defense and offense. Then he makes up plays to exploit those weaknesses.

Goal lines: At each end of the football field is a line marking the scoring area (end zone). That line is the goal line.

Grass Drills: Very strenuous exercises. You run in place a lot, then fall down on the grass and do pushups. Then up and run, then down and do leg lifts. You keep at it till you drop. Good coaches make their teams do grass drills to get them into condition.

Gridiron: Another word for football playing field.

Ground Game: All running plays you make, such as the end sweep, the quarterback sneak, the fullback dive. When you throw passes it's called the "air game" or "passing attack."

Halftime: Midpoint of the game, when the band marches, the twirlers twirl, the team rests in the locker room or on the benches to plan for the second half.

Handoff: During play, when the quarterback gives the football to another offensive player, that's a handoff.

Huddle: Gathering of the team in order to call a play. You circle around each other to keep the defenders from hearing what play you'll try next.

Incomplete Pass: A pass that no one catches.

Intentional Grounding: When you're being rushed by the defense while trying to pass and you throw the ball away from potential interceptors without trying to complete the pass, but solely to avoid being thrown for a loss, the referee calls an intentional grounding penalty. It's totally a judgment call, so quarterback, make your pass look like it's headed for a receiver.

Intercepted Pass: A pass caught by someone on the opposite team instead of by your own receiver.

Jersey: A football-uniform shirt. It usually has a number on it so the crowd can look in the program and see the name of the numbered player. Sometimes jerseys even have the name of the player stitched on them.

Juke Step: A little fakey move to fool whoever tries to tackle you. You juke out of her way.

Kickoff: A free kick, from the 40-yard line, at the start of the game and the start of the second half. Also, after each score, the scoring team kicks off to the team that has been scored on.

Lateral: A backward or sideways pass.

Lateral Pursuit: Running to the side rather than straight ahead.

Linemen: Players who line up close to the line of scrimmage. On offense these players are the center, two guards, two tackles, and two ends.

Line of Scrimmage: An imaginary line that runs from

one side of the field to the other along the path of the ball. Players line up on both sides of the line, facing each other, to begin play.

Long Gainer: A football play that succeeds in getting tons of yards.

Offense: The team that has possession of the ball. The defense is the team that doesn't have possession.

Officials: In a real football game, five men regulate play. They wear black-and-white striped shirts and baseball caps. They watch to see that players keep the rules.

Off Side: You break a rule when you jump across the line of scrimmage before the ball is snapped. Your team loses five yards for being off side.

Off-Tackle Play: A play when the runner blasts outside the opponent's defensive end, sprung off a block by her tackle.

On Side Kickoff: Instead of kicking off as far as you can, kick off just ten yards and try to recover the ball before the other team does.

Pass Pattern: When you run a planned route to catch a pass you're running a pass pattern.

Pitchout: The quarterback takes the hike from center, turns, and tosses the football underhand to his halfback or fullback, who then runs with it.

Place Kick: To kick the football as it is held on the ground by a teammate. You place for a field goal or extra point.

Power Sweep: The Generals' favorite play. It's an end run—the back takes the ball and runs around the defensive end, escorted by two or more blockers.

Punt: To drop the ball and kick it before it hits the ground. You punt to your opponents on fourth down in order to back them up the field away from your goal.

Punt Return: When your opponent punts to your team, one girl catches the ball and runs toward the opponents' goal. Her teammates block for her as she speeds along.

Play Action Pass: The kind of pass when, before the quarterback throws, she fakes a handoff, then steps back to pass.

Pocket: I guess the football pocket is named for a real pocket because they look alike—closed in and comfortable to rest in. In football, when the quarterback drops back behind the center about ten feet to pass, some of her teammates go back with her to defend. They stand by her to keep the defensive team from tackling her before she releases the ball. She's in the pocket.

Press Box: A booth high above the field where the sports reporters and big shots watch the games.

Quarterback Sneak: The quarterback takes the ball from the center and then plunges straight ahead, trying to get between the defenders.

Receivers: Those girls on the offensive team who are eligible to catch a pass, like ends, halfbacks, the fullback.

Rollout: A maneuver by the quarterback when she runs behind the line of scrimmage toward the sidelines, instead of dropping back in the pocket.

Roughing the Passer: Don't do this. When you rush in to drop your opponent's passer, don't hit him, kick him, or anything after he's released the ball. That's too rough, and the ref will slap you with a penalty.

Scrambler: A quarterback who runs around a lot to elude the charging defenders. Usually the quarterback drops back in the pocket; thus she's a drop-back passer. Some quarterbacks prefer to be scramblers. Usually these are short guys who can't see over their linemen, so have to move around to find their receivers.

Screen Pass: In this play the defenders are allowed to

rush the quarterback. But before they get to her, she quickly throws a short pass to a receiver who has drifted behind the oncharging defenders.

Scrimmage: The playing—the action—from the moment the ball is hiked until that down ends.

Scouting Report: You send out a spy to watch the other teams practice or play games. The spy looks for weaknesses. He notices if certain players can't run fast, or if they forget what they're supposed to do, or drop the ball. Then when you play those teams, you take advantage of their weaknesses.

Second Effort: This is when the ball carrier refuses to give up when defenders try to stop her. She keeps plugging away, getting extra yards. Third effort's better. And fourth.

Short Yardage Plays: Plays that gain only a few yards. That's okay. Sometimes you need just a yard or two for a first down.

Shotgun Formation: An offensive formation in which the quarterback stands about five yards behind center, instead of right up behind her. All the other backs and ends run out for a pass instead of blocking for the passer. This gives the quarterback lots of targets.

Sidelines: A line that runs the length of each side of the field marking the boundaries.

Sideline Catch: Pass caught on the sideline. Usually the receiver steps out of bounds after she catches the football. This stops the clock.

Signal: A word, usually a number or "hut, hut," that gets the play started. Quarterbacks call signals.

Sprint Out: To run out fast. To back up fast is called back peddling.

Statue-of-Liberty Play: A really neat play that works like this: The quarterback fades to pass. She holds the ball high over her head, looking like the Statue of

Liberty holding the flaming torch. Then, instead of passing, she drops the ball into the hands of a running back, who takes off for a long gainer.

Stiff Arm or Straight Arm: When you're moving with the football and a tackler comes at you, push out the arm not hanging onto the ball and try to keep the tackler away. Keep your arm rigid.

Sudden Death: When the regular game ends in a tie, a sudden-death overtime can be played. When one team scores, breaking the tie, the game finally ends.

T.D.: A touchdown. Six points scored when you cross the opponent's goal line with the ball.

Tackle: To grab and overpower the ball carrier, throwing her to the ground.

T Formation: A formation where the quarterback lines up exactly behind the center with the fullback just behind her and a halfback on each side. All this is shaped like a T.

Trap Play: When you allow a defender to come through your defensive line, then you block him. Meanwhile your ball carrier runs to the free spot left by the defender.

Yardage: Number of yards gained or lost on a play from scrimmage.

Z-in Pass (Zig In): The receiver sprints downfield about ten yards, then steps toward the middle of the field, then cuts back to the sideline, then back to the middle. She makes a Z.

Zone Block: Very pushy straight-ahead contact between opposing linemen.